# REBIRTH

# REBIRTH

## THE ASCENSION MYTH™ BOOK 5

ELL LEIGH CLARKE

MICHAEL ANDERLE

DISRUPTIVE IMAGINATION

REBIRTH TEAM

*To everyone who ever dreamed of making a dent in the universe.*

*— Ellie*

*To Family, Friends and*
*Those Who Love*
*To Read.*
*May We All Enjoy Grace*
*To Live The Life We Are*
*Called.*

*— Michael*

# ZHYN POLITICIAN

THE KURTHERIAN GAMBIT

# ZHYN SOLDIER

THE KURTHERIAN <sup>(tm)</sup> GAMBIT

© 2016 MICHAEL ANDERLE

# CHAPTER ONE

*ArchAngel,* **Main Lecture Theater**

"Very few people realize quite how many of these genetic relationships exist throughout the galaxies."

The lecture theater was dark and hushed, the audience held in rapt attention.

"In fact, before we had gate technology, there was no way of knowing that these similarities even existed."

The holoslides created a soft glow that bathed the audience in an outline.

Off to one side, the lone professor, seasoned by exposure to the elements and the rougher conditions of cultures across the galaxy, stood delivering his speech to the assembled intellects. His tweed jacket, more for a show of individuality, harked back to the olden days on his planet of ancestry: Earth.

Of course, he hadn't been born there. No one in the Empire had been born there for a good century and a half. But they were comforted knowing that it was still there... back through some gate, somewhere; albeit now just a shell of the civilization their ancestors left behind.

"We've long been able to sequence the genome of a species,"

he continued, "and, of course, certain races visually look the same, giving us further clues."

Professor Giles F. Kurns tapped his fingers together, and the implants registered the action, moving the holoslide animation forward. "What you see on the screen are a male and female Estarian, and a male and female Zhyn." He paused for effect. "I'll let you figure out which is which."

There was a ripple of quiet laughter throughout the audience. He waited a moment, allowing the viewers to compare the footage of the two races standing side by side. His eyes twinkled in the low light. "Pretty astounding similarities, eh?"

He felt more alive when he was either experiencing, or talking about, varied cultures.

Giles wandered up the set of steps in the lecture theater, as the fascinated scientists and students aboard the *ArchAngel* followed him with their eyes. He indicated back at the screen. "You might notice that the main difference is the existence of the bone frill, framing the face of the Zhyn."

He turned and looked at the screen himself, now speaking from amongst the audience. "Now, evolutionary theory explains really well why species evolve a certain way in a closed system. We all know about the old concepts of survival of the fittest. But there is a reason you won't have heard about the Zhyn until about a hundred years ago."

He started walking back down the steps, talking as he went. "Anyone like to have a guess as to why?"

A few hands went up. Giles picked someone over on the other side of the theater, a brunette woman. "Yes, lady in the pink top," he said, gesturing with his outstretched arm, his head down, waiting to hear her answer.

The human turned in her chair and spoke. "We only harnessed gating abilities for exploration and non-military activities a little before that time."

"Excellent!" Giles remarked still without looking up. He continued his descent down the stairs and onto floor level.

"So let me pose a question for you to ponder, next time you're in the shower and contemplating the complexities and vastness of the universe..." His voice lilted up and down, as if he were a shaman mesmerizing them into examining a reality beyond their sheltered existence on the ship.

There were a few chuckles from the audience.

Giles continued, his strange mannerisms and arm gestures punctuating his words as he spoke. "Wonder this..." he paused dramatically. There was silence as they hung on his every word. "Why is it that two seemingly similar races — almost identical in genetic makeup, but for maybe 0.1% of their code — were able to evolve 300 thousand light years away from each other, long before space travel was even a possibility for them? If space travel didn't begin until, say, the last thousand years, how can they have had a few hundred thousand years of separate evolution? And if we're looking at two species in complete isolation, disjoined by geography, is there any real evolution going on here? And if we accept that as a possibility, and remember *they* didn't have space travel, how is it that these two genetically similar races came to be in two different petri dishes floating in space?"

Giles turned and looked at the sea of faces, human and otherwise, all displaying the same look of awe that he got whenever he lectured anywhere.

There was silence; but for the frequency-dependent acoustic dampening in the theater, one could have heard a pin drop.

Giles noticed a slight agitation coming from one of the front rows. A hand went up, hesitantly. "Can you repeat all that, please?"

Giles spun around, searching the lecture theater for something other than the querying hand. "Who here is taking notes?" he asked.

About a quarter of the hands went up.

"'Talk to one of those people with their hands up afterward," he suggested to the person who hadn't been able to keep up, still not looking at him.

"Now…" he continued briskly, "I'm not one for promoting the existence of things for which there's no proof," he paused, using the pitch and pace of his voice to hold the audience. "But for those familiar with Occam's Razor, you may simply assume that there *was* someone capable of space travel. Someone who perhaps gave an Estarian - or a Zhyn - a lift at some point in their history."

He scratched behind his ear and returned to the front bench, adding, "Or maybe a pregnant version of one of them, at least."

Again there were more chuckles from the audience.

Giles flicked theatrically through to his next slide, holding his thumb and forefinger in the air as he tapped them together. "Now, you didn't come here to hear about how wrong Edipus was when he tried to apply Darwinian theory to space history," he smiled, glancing around. "You want to know about the good stuff; the truth in the rumors. The science in the myth… right?"

There were mutters of agreement, and lots of nodding of heads throughout the dimly lit auditorium.

Giles waved his arms in an upward motion. "Well, what if I were to tell you that in our conversation earlier, where we were talking about the Estarian ascension mythology, there was something I left out? A few clues, actually. Clues that would suggest that the ascension phenomena isn't quite as unique as the Estarians would have you believe…"

There were hushed whispers in the darkness as Giles flicked through to another slide, showcasing yet another race that the *ArchAngel* general population wasn't fully aware of.

## CHAPTER TWO

**On Board *The Empress*, Koin Star System, Zhyn Empire, 300 thousand light years from Sark System**

"Twenty minutes!"

There was a bustling of nervous tension throughout the ship. Crash glanced down at the controls, watching carefully as Sean eased back on the velocity.

Sean continued with his announcement. "When we head into orbit, we'll need to be cloaked. But remember: I can't deposit you guys onto the skylift unless we're uncloaked. So you get one chance. You need to get out, and then move, because there's no coming back until Oz takes out the weapons systems."

Joel and Jack looked at each other confidently as they sat in the main lounge in *The Empress*. Joel nodded. "We've got this," he told her.

Jack pursed her lips in determination, and returned the nod before looking over to Paige. "Think it's time to wake the walking Buddha?" she asked, indicating with her head toward the back of the ship.

Paige's look went from anxious to task-mode. "Yes," she

agreed. "She said to give her as long as possible, but I think it's time."

Paige got up from her seat, and headed back to the cargo hold. On her way past, she brushed Pieter's leg, pulling him out of his intense concentration. He looked up and saw Jack looking back at him.

Jack smiled. "You guys almost ready?" she asked.

Pieter nodded. "Yep. Oz is confident. And if all goes according to plan, we'll be good."

Joel stood up, stretched, and started warming up his muscles by moving around. "It will all go according to plan," he told them, back in Space Marine mode. "And if it doesn't, we'll kill whatever we have to until it does."

Jack grinned, feeling the tension in her own body break. "And that's just how we roll, eh? Mr. Don't-Fuck-With-Me?"

Joel nodded. "That is how we roll. We work for the Queen Bitch, now. We have standards to uphold."

Jack felt a sense of pride swell in her chest as he said that. She glanced back at Pieter, and his smile suggested he was feeling the same way.

Paige came striding back down the aisles between the anti-grav chairs. She was raising her eyes to the heavens.

Joel watched her returning. "What's up?" he asked, concern in his voice.

Paige tried to hide her grin. "Her ladyship is jonesing for a mocha! Of all times!"

Joel grinned as he started checking his weapons and strapping on the additional pieces of body armor that had been sitting one seat over from he and Jack. "I thought it made her nauseous?"

Paige shook her head. "So did I. But, apparently, she wants some."

Paige strode past the group and over into the far corner of the lounge where there was a custom-built mocha machine. In all their time training and performing simulations, it had become apparent that any time spent on the ship was going to require mochination of the highest quality. And so, Brock was instructed to install a state-of-the-art mocha machine, which didn't rely on gravity for it to work.

"I mean, you wouldn't expect us to go without restrooms, would you?" Molly had justified when she broached the subject in one of their team meetings.

Back in the cockpit, Sean and Crash remained focused on the flying. Crash had clocked about 40 hours on *The Empress* in the last week, but wasn't feeling confident enough to take primary. Sitting next to Sean, his attention now on the controls of the ship — rather than the navigation he'd managed to help with — his attention was unyielding.

Sean pointed to another holo representation. "Okay, now we want to drop out of warp," he told Crash, waving his finger at the dial next to a graphic of some kind of warp engine, before knocking the dial down.

He paused for a moment, thinking. "And then, we want to maintain our course, which means...?" He glanced over at Crash for an answer, pausing his actions so as not to give away the next move.

Crash thought fast. "Which means... we need to kick in with the boosters on automatic course correction, to counter the directionality of falling out of warp drive."

Sean made the necessary switch, and slowly brought the boosters online, engaging them at 80%.

Crash sighed in relief, realizing only then that he had been holding his breath.

Sean glanced over to him briefly before looking back at the console. "It's okay. You're doing great, mate."

Crash bobbed his head, his wrinkled forehead showing how uncertain he still felt. Flying had always been his superpower. He'd been flying the weirdest and most dangerous ships and missions all his grown up life. And yet, navigating *The Empress* was a challenge he never thought he'd face.

A female voice interrupted their conversation over the audio feed. "Sean, are you ready for an update on maneuvering into orbit?"

Sean flicked another switch without taking his eyes from his panel. "Yes, please, Emma" he replied.

"Okay then," Emma responded. A new screen overlaid the main window in the space ahead of them. "We are sixteen minutes from joining their orbit. The planet has fifteen space lifts, and there are twenty-three satellites in orbit. Plus one space station. I have plotted the optimal route which will bypass their normal routes into orbit, so we will mostly avoid contact with any other vessel."

Sean frowned. "Mostly?" he clarified.

"77% mostly," Emma replied.

Sean's frown deepened. "Is that the best we can do?" he asked.

Emma's voice was firm. "Given the parameters, yes."

Sean wasn't convinced. "So if we end up colliding with another vessel in orbit, or on approach...?" he asked.

Emma responded immediately. "Envelope maneuvers, baby," she told him. "I know it's what you like."

Sean grinned to himself as Crash watched him. "Oh, Emma, you little minx. You know me so well."

Emma's face came onto the video feed in the corner of his console. "Well, I find it helps with keeping you in line. And FYI, I shared my heuristics of you with Ozymandeus for his people-behavior project."

Sean shook his head in disbelief. "Women! Can't you ever keep your secrets to yourselves?"

Emma smiled on the video feed and responded calmly. "Not when it comes to our fellow entity intelligences, no."

Sean grinned. "Right, I'm going to make sure that these rogues out back are ready to jump. Crash, can you keep Emma company for me, please?"

Crash was still deep in concentration. He woke himself, breaking his gaze from the panel he had been watching. "Sure," he agreed, his face just as expressionless as ever.

Sean left the cockpit and wandered through the narrow passageway into the lounge area. He arrived in the doorway to see Joel and Jack doing their final prep. "Someone told Molly it's time?" he checked, mild concern on his face; he was worried that she might be sleeping.

Paige looked up from her holo. "She's-"

"Right here," Molly finished her sentence, appearing at the back of the lounge. She was in full combat gear, ready to go, holding her wooden baton. Her face was eerily peaceful, and her manner relaxed.

Paige spun around in her chair to look at her. "Mocha is just brewing," she told her, indicating over to the machine.

Sean looked at Molly, then at the mocha machine. "Will you never learn?" he asked her. His tone resembled how a parent would talk to a child.

Molly held his gaze as she strode deliberately through the lounge. Sean suddenly felt strangely intimidated by her presence and her quietness. Give him geeky Molly. Give him matter-of-fact Molly. Give him amped-up, kicking-his-ass-across-the-gym Molly. But meditating Molly... He couldn't get a read on her.

She got close to where he had planted himself at the end of one of the aisles. Feeling her come closer, he was unable to stay where he was. He took a couple of paces backwards, and Molly walked straight past him to the mocha machine.

It had stopped pouring mocha into the antigrav mug beneath, and she picked it up, taking in the aroma and savoring the smell. Joel and Jack had turned to look at her, and were watching her enjoy the moment of her first mocha after a long meditation session. She breathed it in, and then gently took a sip. She exhaled slowly in pleasure.

Turning around, she smiled at the crew. "So, what are we doing standing around, bitches? Don't we have a mission to complete?"

Joel and Jack snapped into action and headed straight toward the back of the ship. Paige looked flustered. "Are you okay?" she asked.

Molly was midway through another sip of mocha. She nodded, her nose still in the mug. She finished her sip, and pulled her talisman from around her neck, showing it to Paige. "Thanks to this, I am," she smiled.

Paige's face relaxed a little. "And no shifting while you were back there?"

Molly shook her head. "Nope. All mundane and grounded in this reality," she confirmed. She took another gulp of mocha before setting the mug to the side. Molly looked back at Sean. "Look after that for me?" she asked him.

Sean nodded. "Sure. Just get your ass back up here, pronto," he said, relaxing a little now that she was returning to her normal self.

"I'll do my best," she said, smiling at him before taking off to join Jack and Joel down at the drop point.

Paige watched her leave. As soon as she was out of earshot, she turned back to Sean. "Please tell me this is a good idea? Letting her go down there like this. In her condition."

Sean shrugged. "She's the boss. I can't stop her."

Paige frowned, looking anxious again. "What about the General?"

Sean shook his head slowly. "He made a judgment call. She's in better physical shape than any of us. She's sharper than she's ever been, and he can't see that the pod doc would have done anything bad to her. They've got a few hundred years of data to back up the concept that it only enhances, so we've got to believe that whatever she's going through is an... enhancement."

Paige folded her arms. "An enhancement that might just get her - and everyone down there with her - killed."

Sean took a deep breath. "I'm sure they'll be fine; Joel is with her. And besides, since the meditating has been helping her control the realm jumping, she's probably got a few hours before she's at risk again."

Paige slumped back into her seat with a 'humph'. "Let's hope so," she said, looking pointedly at Sean like it was his fault.

Sean shook his head in defeat, knowing better than to argue with her. "I'm going to make sure they get away okay," he said. "Pieter, let me know when you guys are online. I'll come and sit with you for the next piece."

Pieter grunted his agreement as Sean strode away. Paige turned in her seat to talk to Pieter, whose eyes remained glued to his holo. Seeing he was mission-focused, she thought better of airing her grievances with him, and turned back to sit in her seat quietly.

### ArchAngel, Main Lecture Theater

Giles completed his lecture. "Thank you," he said, and paused. "Class dismissed!" He waved his hand and bowed subserviently to his audience.

A round of applause erupted from the theater. Though they had some of the best minds in the Empire assembled here, the scientific and student communities were always moved by the charisma and charm exuded by this strange professor who would duck in with a guest lecture series every few years.

There were rumors that he was commissioned by the General to research the paranormal. Other whispers suggested that the anthropology was just a cover so that he could go off traveling and exploring. Some thought that he was a spy, looking out for the Empire's interests, deftly protecting them while pretending to be this middle-aged geek with oddities; the tweed jacket with arm patches was all part of his act to appear non-threatening.

Right now, though, no one cared. Several audience members were already on their feet applauding. The younger generations were cheering and whooping, wondering why the heck their regular professors couldn't be so damn interesting.

Giles raised a hand in thanks and bowed again. Eventually, the cheering and clapping subsided; but no one moved, apart from a few students in the front rows, who were scrambling to gather their things and line up to talk with him. Giles ignored them for a moment and informally addressed the theater. "Alright, folks, that's all I got. Class dismissed!"

Still no one moved. "That means bugger off to the bar! I'll be right behind you. Mine is a tequila," he told them. "Neat. No ice."

There was a ripple of laughter, and finally people started gathering their things and filing out through the doors at the back.

Giles sighed, smiling contentedly to himself. His holo buzzed, and he held up his index finger to the student who was first in line to speak with him.

The message was from ADAM.

THE GENERAL WOULD LIKE TO SEE YOU BEFORE YOU LEAVE FOR YOUR NEXT 'EXCURSION'.

Giles smiled and typed his response back.

WHAT'S WITH THE FUCKING QUOTATION MARKS?!! >> SEND.

An instant later, another message came through from ADAM.

COME ON. WE ALL KNOW THAT YOUR 'RESEARCH' IS JUST AN EXCUSE TO JOLLY AROUND THE GALAXY UNDER DIPLOMATIC PRIVILEGES. ;) ANYWAY, WOULD DINNER TOMORROW EVENING WORK FOR YOU?

Giles grinned, a flush of humor bubbling up as laughter in his throat. He was aware of his students watching him, so he hurried his response.

OF COURSE. I'D BE HONORED. LET ME KNOW WHERE AND WHEN AND I'LL MAKE MYSELF AVAILABLE. >> SEND

Giles looked up at the first expectant student in the queue, and then along the line that had formed. There were at least twenty people he needed to talk to.

"Hi," he said to the first one, as the student pulled up his holo notes to ask their question.

# CHAPTER THREE

**On Board *The Empress*, Koin Star System, In orbit around Planet Kurilia**

Joel grunted as he put the hatch into manual mode. "Force-field is still intact, so we should be okay to open her up and drop through whenever we're ready," he told Jack.

Jack watched in awe as the hatch began to open up to reveal space beneath them. The hatch was about four feet by four feet: plenty big enough for them just to fit through. As it opened, a frame came down from above, dropping beyond the hole in the ship and extending by a few feet. She pointed at it. "What's that for?" she asked Joel.

Emma came online. "That's to help you navigate down through the hole."

Jack frowned. "In the Space Marines, they just had us jump."

Emma's tone was matter-of-fact. "That is fine when you're using an antigrav suit, or when you have a whole field to land in; but when you're trying to hit an elevator lift deck, it's prudent to move more precisely."

Jack and Joel exchanged looks, and Jack smiled. "Well, that's me told!" she exclaimed.

Just then Molly walked in, followed closely by Sean. "Wow, we have a climbing frame!" she grinned. "This ship just gets better and better." She started arranging her body armor, and closing up the straps and pockets. "There I was, thinking we were going to have to do the trust jump like in Space Cadets."

Jack smiled back at her. "Yes, better we have a more precise landing, given that the elevator platform is so small."

Joel looked at Jack with humor in his eyes. He remained silent.

Molly turned to Sean as he followed her into the room. "Is this ship going to get us close enough to the platform?" she asked him.

Sean raised his voice a little, and looked across the room. "Emma? How close can you get us?"

Emma's audio cracked on again. "Within five feet, plus or minus two feet tolerance."

Sean looked at Molly with the answer. Molly nodded. "Perfect; barely a drop at all. As long as nothing moves."

Joel moved over to the climbing frame. "Right, all looks good. Is Oz ready?" he asked, glancing up at Molly.

**Yes. Ready to rock.**

Molly nodded. "He's all kinds of ready," she smiled, peering over the edge of the hatch into the blackness.

Emma chimed into the conversation. "Okay, we're decreasing our altitude. You should see the platform come into view within the next forty seconds."

The team started to feel the effects of the gravity of the planet as their orbit changed, and they approached the sky lift. Just then, the platform came into one corner of the view the hatch afforded them.

Joel looked up. "Alright folks, listen up." He was in ops mode. "Jack, you're up first. Then Molly. Then I'll follow you both down."

He looked up at Sean. "Sean, you do your one orbit, and then expect us back here, at this same lift. If we're not there, you know the next one to check. If we're not there, and you can't reach us through Oz or the quantum comm, then you need to get *The Empress* out of here, and leave us."

Sean nodded. "Got it. Just make sure you don't put me in that position," he told Joel seriously. Sean leaned forward and shook Joel's hand, clamping him on the shoulder firmly.

Jack was holding onto the frame with both hands, ready to start her descent. Sean moved past her out of the way, but patted her on the back, too. She turned her head to acknowledge him. "You be careful down there," he told her. "And if you can't be careful, be ruthless."

She nodded. "See you in one orbit," she said, pursing her lips. With that, she swung underneath the bar she was holding onto, and put her feet on a rung opposite her before turning herself around and climbing down.

The platform was coming closer.

Emma made another announcement. "Okay, we're at our slowest rate now. We will continue to cruise at this speed, and by my calculations you have about five seconds to get onto the platform before we move out of range.

Molly swung herself onto the frame. "We've all got to go at once," she declared.

Joel swung down onto the frame, too. "Looks like," he agreed. "Okay, stay close. We can do this." The three of them looked at each other in solidarity as the platform came closer.

Sean squatted down next to Molly. She had one arm wrapped around the frame, just a few feet off the basement floor. Sean put his hand on her arm. "You be extra careful," he told her. "Remember your breathing, and stay focused. We need you back in one piece."

Molly nodded. "I will. I promise."

The metal platform with the tiny hut that housed the skylift now blocked out the view of the planet and the clouds beneath.

Joel took hold of a bar in the middle of the hatch's frame, and shouted to the other two. "Okay, let's move. Go! GO! GO!"

Jack disappeared from the frame first. She landed, and rolled on the platform before scrambling up and out of the way. Molly dropped next. Then Joel. Sean saw them each land, and watched as long as he could before they were obscured behind the little building. He watched the whole structure disappear from view of the hatch.

"Okay, Emma, they're gone. Let's close her up, and keep an eye out for their comm signal," he told her. "And let me know as soon as you have them."

The frame retracted, and the hatch started to close.

"You'll be the first to know, Sean," Emma assured him.

Sean stood up and stepped away from the closing hatch. He had been wearing his ops face, but now, finding himself alone in the bowels of the ship, his mask dropped, and the anxiety became evident around his eyes.

He rubbed his face with both hands, and stood staring into space for a moment, hoping that Molly really was going to be okay.

**On Board *The Empress***

Crash sat back in his console chair, watching the screen Emma had just pulled up. "So when you get a comm connection with them, it will show up as a signal here?"

"Exactly," Emma replied. "It's just a matter of time." Her EI voice filled the spacious clinical-looking cockpit as Crash grappled to try and understand the extensive functionality on the ship. For starters, he was still getting used to Emma; Sean had introduced her as the Entity Intelligence, or EI, that ran *The Empress*.

"The quantum connection," Emma explained, "means that it's location independent; there's nothing to interfere. It just takes a little while for it to come online; but its accuracy is much better once the comms are away from the quantum field created by the gate generator. That's why we don't activate them while they're still on board."

Crash took a deep breath. "There's just so much to know."

Emma's tone was sympathetic. "It's okay. You'll get there. I mean, you're flying on forty hours of training. Did Sean not tell you how long most pilots need on simulation mode before they're fit to fly solo?"

Crash shook his head, and then realized that Emma probably wasn't able to see him. "No?" he confirmed, vocally.

"Try three years of twenty hours a week!" she exclaimed. "Sean was a slow one. He had to retake most of the tests twice, so he was three and a half years in simulations before they ever let him loose to take off!"

Crash sat up straighter. "Seriously? He never mentioned that. I've been feeling like I'm a slowpoke!"

"Seriously," Emma confirmed. "He's a sly one, that Royale; not even telling you the length of the training…"

Sean stepped into the cockpit. "Giving away more of my secrets there, Emma?"

"Just helping your protégé gain some perspective," Emma replied without a hint of guilt.

"Right," he said flatly.

Crash turned to look at him. "Why didn't you tell me that? Three years, man!"

Sean grinned. "Because, young man, you will not need that long. The rate you're going, you'll be flying solo in a month. That's flying with minimal EI capabilities. If, somehow, I get wiped out and the ship is still flying, you would need 3,000 hours to get up to speed."

Crash's head moved back involuntarily. "Really?" he asked, his face still relatively unchanged despite his surprise.

Sean bobbed his head as he pulled his console chair around

and climbed back in. "Sure. You're a natural. One of the most talented I've ever seen. You intuitively understand how the tech works, so you only need showing once... You'll have this down in no time."

Crash relaxed back in his chair. This time his face seemed a little lighter than it had.

There was movement in the passageway. The two pilots turned to see Brock stumbling through the door.

Sean spun his chair around to face him properly. "All okay back there?"

Brock was panting dramatically. "Yeah..." he said, pushing his way into the cockpit and pulling one of the other six chairs around. He climbed up and sat back. "Ahhhhh..." he breathed, closing his eyes. "That's better."

Sean raised one eyebrow, still looking at him.

Brock felt the weight of Sean's gaze, and opened one eye. He sat up a little and opened both eyes. "Okay. So you probably want an update?"

Sean nodded. "That would be... helpful."

Brock sighed and shifted a little more upright in his console chair. "Okay, so it was tough work, but I managed to recalibrate the frequency of the shield to mask the data transmissions that Oz will be using. It effectively blinds their systems." He paused, and looked pointedly at Sean. "Do you have any idea how difficult it was to do that?"

Sean smiled. "No. But it sounds complex."

Brock lay back again, waving his hand. "Man, you have no idea, especially given the short window we had!" He closed his eyes again. "But it's done."

Sean chuckled and turned back to his console, shaking his head.

Crash had started to relax a little, while still keeping one eye on the quantum comm signal screen. "What I still don't fully understand is why the General has us doing this mish. I mean, doesn't he have better trained, more capable teams at his disposal in the Etheric Empire?"

Brock opened one eye again. "'More capable'? Speak for yourself, baby!" He smiled to himself and closed his eye.

Crash's lips turned up at the corners ever so slightly.

Sean rubbed the stubble on his face. "He does," he said, carefully watching Brock for a reaction before continuing. "Only there are political things at play. He can't be seen to be forcibly decommissioning or constraining a planet's military right now - even if they are secretly and illegally arming themselves up beyond the official agreement. And if his people were caught doing it, there would be hell to pay."

Crash frowned. "So, what, we're the clandestine team that gives him deniability?"

Sean pushed his lips out. "Yeah. Something like that," he agreed. "The General is under pressure to reduce his forces — except he knows that this is just a ploy to leave the Empire defenseless so that other parties can come in and take them out. Only…" Sean looked a little shifty and lowered his voice. "He's not meant to know that, and revealing that he does will cause big problems. So, basically, what we're doing cannot be traced back to the Etheric Empire under any circumstances."

Brock laid motionless, his eyes still closed. "So what about that big fuck-off logo on the side of the ship? And the pretty picture of our esteemed Empress?"

Sean grinned. "Yeah. That."

Crash looked at Sean. "Yeah, won't it be recognized?"

Sean glanced at the console at his right elbow. "You want to explain this bit, Emma?"

Emma's audio channel opened with a tiny crack. "Sure. The forcefield has various settings. Mostly, we used it to deflect radar devices, as well as physical attacks. Then, about sixty years ago, a bright young thing on Lance's team came up with the idea of having our cloaks actually be visual. She seemed to like to use ships in close contact with the enemies, so they had a team develop a kind of visual camouflaging ability. We can pretty much make the outside of the ship look like anything we want. Right now, we appear the same as the commercial ships coming and going from the planet's surface."

Crash wiped his face with his hand. "That's... amazing."

"Yeah," agreed Emma. "It's pretty cool."

Crash's lips did their turny-uppy thing at the edges again. Sean noticed Crash's amusement at Emma, and remembered that these Sarkians hadn't been around EIs at all until Oz jumped right past and went straight to an AI.

"Okay," Sean said, changing the subject and checking his console again. "Let's see if we can get a read-out on those miscreants down on the surface yet."

### Planet Kurilia, Capital Building of the Zhyn Empire

Lord High Marshall Shaa remained bolt upright at his desk. His blue skin caught the light from the floor-to-ceiling panels, which transmitted varying amounts of the radiation at different times of the day. Right now, it was almost noon for the planet Kurilia; meaning that only 20% of the radiation was being let through the active biofilter, permitting optimal environmental conditions.

As the head of the entire Zhyn military, Lord High Marshall Shaa was used to being the most powerful person in any room. And he expected due deference.

Now he regarded his subordinate, standing several feet in front of his desk. "Why is it, Justicar Beno'or, that every time I send you with a mandate to this Reynolds human, you come back without an agreement?"

Diplomatic Affairs Justicar Beno'or fidgeted awkwardly as he stood before the High Marshall. Shaa's Vice High Marshall looked on quietly from the other side of the room; he managed to maintain a look of neutrality from many years in high office, where it was always best to keep one's personal feelings concealed. He was looking down at his hands, which were neatly folded in his lap.

Beno'or scratched at the side of his head, just behind the boney frill that framed his face, thinking of how to position what he still needed to relay.

"Well?" Shaa growled, his impatience showing.

Beno'or took a deep breath. "Well, Your Highness..." he paused, checking himself briefly. "It appears that the underlying problem may be that Reynolds doesn't intend to disarm at all."

Shaa looked about to explode.

At that moment, his right hand man chose to inject himself into the conversation. "If I may, Your Highness?" he asked, standing and walking towards the fearful looking Justicar. "Whether Reynolds intends to play ball or not, if he wants unity, he's going to have to agree to our terms."

He paused, glancing at Beno'or, knowing that it was prudent not to share much of their plan with him. Ever. "When Reynolds discovers that the others are ready to be involved, if he wants to avoid the weight of their military might, he will have to comply."

He shifted his glance from Beno'or to his master, and then lowered his eyes again in respect.

Shaa looked somewhat appeased as he exhaled slightly. "This is true." He pushed back his chair slightly, and looked to Beno'or again. "I expect you to try again within the moon. Leave us, now," he commanded dismissively.

Beno'or, freed from the anxious torment, found his feet and made his way as quickly as he could from the grand office. His footsteps clunked clumsily across the carbon-fiber tiles, making far more noise than the calculated precise steps of Vice High Marshall Davon.

Shaa indicated to the scuttling Zhyn, as he sat back in the

chair a little more comfortably, now that he was in private. "What do you make of that?" he asked his trusted advisor.

Davon approached the desk a little closer than Beno'or had dared venture. "I think he's perceptive. Or he has intel." He looked down at his nails casually. "Either way, I'll find out. If he's right, then these talks will probably need spicing up a little."

Shaa sneered. "What did you have in mind?" he asked.

Davon maintained his polite composure. "I believe a show of strength and unity would perhaps force Reynolds to reconsider. Just enough to show him that we are better as friends than we are as enemies."

Shaa nodded. "Well, if it was just brute force, we could have done that already. We decided long ago that we need them to demilitarize before we would be a match for them."

Davon nodded. "But now, with *The Empress* gone, rumor has it that there is unrest in the Empire. And with our other partners, I don't believe this Reynolds is capable of standing firm under such pressure. He's a politician now. Not a warrior."

Shaa looked contemplative, absorbing what he was being told. "I agree. No real General leaves military command to take a political position, as he did. Not unless he's lost the stomach for war."

He paused before pulling himself back to the matter at hand. "So you believe he'll concede for the sake of peace?"

Davon paused, carefully considering his words. "I think he'll weigh the considerations carefully," he said. "For the most part, our technological abilities are almost evenly matched, from what our scouts can find. However, *they* are much larger. We have three worlds' worth of excellent raw materials and military talent to draw from. Plus, when was the last time that they really went to war — without *The Empress* driving the initiative?" he clarified.

Shaa shook his head. They both knew the answer to that.

Davon concluded his assessment. "All things considered, I believe we need to pursue the diplomatic channels publicly, but continue our covert efforts; then see if we can add some additional pressure that we can deny knowledge of, but which sends a very clear message."

Shaa puffed his chest a little as he took a deep breath. "I agree. As much as I'd like to show them who they are dealing with overtly, going up against a smaller fleet would be strategically sensible."

Davon didn't move a muscle. He stood in front of his commander, awaiting instructions.

Shaa was still deep in thought. "You make some interesting points," he said. "See if you can set up a meeting with the others. If we're going to do this, we need to make sure that we're not acting alone."

Davon snapped to attention and bowed. "Very good, Your Highness. I will make the arrangements."

Shaa spun his chair around to look out onto the surface of the planet, beyond his primary military base. He watched the nearby skylift whizzing up and down, taking personnel to and from the orbiting space stations and waiting craft. His military might was formidable, and growing in secret.

But his military was not yet enough to rival the Etheric Empire, or as they were calling themselves now, the Etheric Federation. Reynolds was having to focus on all of the challenges with bringing together different alien races into one group with the Etheric Empire still the most powerful among them.

*With a little political maneuvering, though...*

A smile crept across his deep blue lips as he contemplated potential victories.

# CHAPTER FOUR

**<u>Planet Kurilia, Perimeter of PrimeBase, Northern Hemisphere</u>**

"We need to get into that building." Molly frowned, peeking at their target from the last of their tree cover.

Joel scanned the area looking for a break in the fence that surrounded the base. "We've no pods to perform our usual break-in antics…" He pulled his lips to one side, thinking.

Jack kept her eyes peeled for any sign of people. The last thing they needed was to be rumbled before they got what they came for.

Molly seemed to have made a decision, though. She straightened up and pulled her baton out from between the holsters on her back.

"I'm going in," she announced, "the old-fashioned way."

Joel looked at her with a hint of sarcasm on his face. "Seriously? With a wooden stick?"

"No," she smiled as if to call him silly. "Hold it for me," she said, handing it to him. She started taking off her weapons and relinquishing them to Jack and Joel.

"I'm going to get into their data center, and it will be easier if I don't look like the Terminator."

Jack looked confused. "How? They have retinal scans and all sorts of security checks. Not to mention you're... erm... small and monkey-like."

Molly grinned. "You mean human?" She laughed a little. "It's just like anything based on relationships... I'm going to have to see about playing to my advantages. And remember — no one expected the Spanish Inquisition..."

Joel eyed her, worried.

Her voice trailed off as the faces of her comrades showed they had spent zero hours watching the old television archives from Earth. She shook her head in dismay and finished stripping her gear off. She looked almost civilian in her one-piece, leathers, and combat boots.

She pulled her hair tie out and ruffled her brown hair a little. "Okay," she announced, "wish me luck!"

Joel watched her walk away from their hiding place in the trees, and over to a gate in the fence. He couldn't fathom what she was possibly going to do.

*When did Molly have an advantage regarding relationships?*

Jack also watched her go. "That lady sure has balls of steel," she commented to Joel, a hint of admiration in her voice.

Molly slipped through the fence and approached the target building. She saw a scientist in a lab coat disappearing into the server entrance; then she spotted another person walking across the concrete open area, heading for the same door. She ambled over as casually as she could.

The Zhyn in the white coat looked up at her. This was the first time Molly had seen this blue-skinned race; though many of their features resembled that of the Estarians on her home planet, their faces were framed like the triceratops she learned about from Earth's history archives. Their eyes were mesmerizing, too — golden, with flecks of light that seemed to emanate from them.

She tried not to stare.

**If you stare, he'll know that you're not from around here.**

*And the pink skin and human features don't give me away?*

**Yeah. You're going to need to play it casual.**

*Yeah, yeah; use his surprise to keep him off-guard. Tap into social norms, etc.*

**Exactly.**

*I just hope the social norms that we know are the same as what he knows.*

**Yeah, good luck with that.**

*Thanks, Oz. Very helpful.*

Molly approached the stranger, her hands by her sides and her lips smiling softly. "Greetings!" she called out to him.

He looked immediately uncertain. He tried to look away, but Molly was heading straight for him.

"Hey," Molly persisted. "I was wondering if you could help me?"

*Oz. Have you done something? I feel a little strange when I speak.*

**Just helping out with the language translation. You're now speaking Zhyn, with an Entruvian regional dialect.**

*No shit?!*

**Shit.**

*Thanks, Oz. Great move.*

**At your service.**

The scientist slowed his pace and looked at Molly. "Hello," he said, his accent lilting a little.

She put her weight on one leg and allowed her hip to stick out a little, making her seem less formidable.

"I feel so silly asking you this," she began, now that she knew he was listening, "but I'm here on an exchange mission, and I need to meet my boss in there."

She pointed back towards the data center. She lowered her

eyes and blushed a little. "Except I left my access pass inside, and I'm not set up on the system, yet." She signaled to her eyes, referring to the retinal scan. "I don't suppose you could help me get back in, could you?"

The man regarded her warily, looking around. "I'm not sure. It would be a breach of security."

Molly looked down. "Ah, yes. I understand." She turned as if to go, and slapped her hand on her forehead. "I'm so stupid!" she added, muttering to herself.

The man took a step in her direction, before heading towards the door again. He watched her carefully. "You know... It's okay. I can let you in this once."

Molly smiled to herself.

**Nicely done, Ms. Bates. I can see you have mastered "the old-fashioned way..."**

*Why, thank you, Oz. And yes, years of getting into labs I didn't have clearance for. There's almost a geek code.*

The man led the way towards the building, Molly striding confidently after him.

He stood by the holo panel and waved his hand, activating the panel to scan his eyes. The door slid open, and he waved for her to go in ahead of him.

"Thank you," she said graciously. Or at least that was what she thought she said. Her lips and mouth were indeed making different, unfamiliar movements.

**It's okay. You'll get used to it.**

*I hope so. This is weird.*

The scientist followed her in, their eyes adjusting to the lower light levels. "What is your supervisor called?" he asked.

Molly slapped her head again. "Oh, you're going to think that I'm so stupid. It was my first time meeting him earlier. I can't remember."

The man looked even more suspicious than previously.

"It's okay," she recovered quickly. "I'll find him. Thanks so much for your help."

He bowed slightly, and she returned the bow. He turned to leave, and Molly did the same, walking in the opposite direction.

*Oz, I need a schematic, and directions to the nearest Server point for access.*

**Working on it. I just have to get into their systems.**

There was a pause.

**Okay. I'm in.**

Molly turned back and noticed that the scientist was walking off down the corridor along the front of the building. He turned to look at her. She waved awkwardly, and he turned away again, continuing on his journey.

**Okay, you need to head straight into the heart of the building. So straight on from where we came in the door.**

Molly walked into the dimly-lit foyer, which opened up into a larger hall. It was all wood paneled — nothing like any military operation she'd seen in the Sark System.

**Straight on. Through the hall, and into the corridor on the other side.**

Molly felt exposed as she walked through, her footsteps echoing loudly no matter how softly she trod. There were three people huddled together in one corner, deep in a discussion. As she walked past, she drew their attention; but she kept walking.

Seeing the door now, her eyes adjusting somewhat, her heart started to race as she neared her first goal.

**Once in the corridor, you want to follow it down to another set of doors.**

*Oz? Don't I need security clearance?*

**Already handled. I'm on their network now.**

Molly sighed in relief as the doors slid open in front of her. She stepped through into a more brightly lit corridor. It was stark and clinical. She couldn't tell what kind of building materials had been used; some looked natural, like wood, where others looked like wood-plastic hybrids. The light was soft, and she tried to identify the source as she hurriedly made her way through the passage.

About twenty paces ahead of her was another set of doors.

**That's it. Just through there are the servers. The nearest point for us to plug into is to the right as you go in the door. Fourth stack down.**

Molly breathed and focused as she covered the last few paces to the door. *Nearly there,* she told herself.

"Hey, you!" a voice called out behind her.

She spun around to see another Zhyn in a military uniform heading her way.

He was armed. She kept walking.

"Stop right there!" the voice called again.

Molly turned around. "Huh? Me?" she asked, pointing to herself.

*Oz, get me out of this one!*

"Yes, you. Hands up," the man commanded, pointing his weapon at her.

Molly slowly raised her hands up above her shoulders. "Have I done something wrong?" she asked.

The guard slowed, looking a little confused. "What are you doing here?"

She pointed over her shoulder, in the direction of the doors at the end of the corridor. "I'm going to meet my supervisor. He said he'd meet me in there about now. I'm here on exchange, a diplomatic exchange, for the data convention next month."

Her detainer looked even more confused, but then he straightened. "I need to check out your story. Until then, you're coming with me."

*Oz?*

**Nearly there.**

The Zhyn's expression shifted, and he seemed to be changing his mind. A second later, he lowered his weapon.

*Oz?*

I've just given him a message on his eye display that makes it seem like his system ran a facial recognition of you. You're now in their system as a diplomatic exchange scientist. Your supervisor's name is Xcli'tr.

*Say that again?*

'Els-i-ter' would work, if you wanted to say it in a human accent.

*Got it. Els-ister.*

**Near enough.**

The guard addressed her again. "Sorry ma'am. You're free to go."

Molly bowed her head. "Thank you," she said quietly.

The doors opened behind her, and she strode the rest of the way down the corridor and through into the server room, as fast as she reasonably could without looking suspicious.

*Mother of all fucks! That was close.*

**Yeah. Well, you do insist on getting yourself into these scrapes.**

*I guess it's all risk compensation, Oz. I know I've got you to get me out of them if I get stuck.*

Oz chuckled, making Molly's head hum a little.

Molly turned right and headed into the server stacks. She counted off. *One, two...*

She kept walking, her feet barely making a sound on the rubber carpet.

*Three, four.*

She rounded the corner and stepped into the aisle between the servers. She could feel the heat coming off of them, and the air system extracting as much of the heat from the room as possible. It made for hot and cold patches of air all over the place.

**You want the one that matches the symbol we practiced. It's probably a port that is fairly obvious and accessible. They**

**use this to pull data and download updates, from what ADAM told me.**

Molly searched through the machines, looking for any kind of port that had the circle surrounded by eight attached circles. It took a few minutes, but she managed.

*Got it.*

**Okay. You know what to do.**

Molly inserted the dongle into the port, and pushed it in as far as it would go.

*Has that done it?*

Oz was silent for a second.

**Yes, that's it. We're all good. I just need thirty seconds.**

Molly's mouth twitched. *This is sounding more and more like a date.*

**What?**

*Nothing.*

Molly looked around, taking in as much detail as she could. *Thirty seconds to kill...* she thought.

She crept back to the end of the stack and peered around the corner to see if anyone else was nearby. She couldn't see anyone, but there were sounds like people were moving around somewhere on the other side of the server room.

She noticed the quantum bead in her wrist was illuminated; that meant she was connected. She pressed it, and pulled up her holo.

IN SERVER ROOM. PATCH UPLOADING. COMING BACK IN 20S.>>Send.

The quantum bead under the skin in her wrist lit up a little more, and then returned to its previous glow.

*Message sent, I guess.*

She wandered back to the dongle and stood in front of it, waiting to pull it out. Suddenly, she heard voices by the door. She kept still, trying to listen, but she couldn't make out the words.

**Okay. We're good to go.**

Molly pulled out the dongle and slid it carefully back into her pocket. Then she headed back to the end of the stack, slowly peering out from behind the banks of machines before committing herself to stepping out.

The voices seemed to have moved off in the other direction, leaving her free to extract herself via the door she'd come in. Carefully, she made her way to the exit, as quickly as she could.

There were two scientists just off to the right, working at a console with their backs to the door. They were talking in low voices.

*Okay, this isn't ideal, but I'm going for it.*

**Door is ready when you are.**

*Let's do it.*

Molly strode out quietly but casually, heading for the open door that was about ten paces ahead of her, but across an exposed area.

She could see the corridor beyond.

"Excuse me! Who are you, and what are you doing in here?" a voice behind her boomed out.

*Fuck. Fuck, fuck, fuck, fuck, fuck.*

**It's okay. We've got this. You're on their system. Be cool, girl. Be cool.**

Molly turned around to face her questioner. An older male Zyhn was walking toward her, looking displeased.

A female hung back, watching what was happening.

"Greetings," Molly began. "I'm—"

The scientist interrupted her. "Not meant to be in here!" he told her. "Who are you?" he demanded.

He was larger than the other Zhyn she had seen. He had the height of an Estarian, but he had more features of an Ogg; the waistline, specifically.

"I'm Sandra," Molly said, trying to sound casual. "I'm here on a diplomatic data exchange. I was going to meet my supervisor in here, but then I forgot something."

"And who, pray tell, is your supervisor?" he demanded.

"Els-ister," she answered after only a slight hesitation.

The man looked thoughtful. Then he looked amused as he tapped something on his hand, which was presumably linked to his eye display.

He turned his attention back to Molly. "Well, *Sandra*; since I am *'Els-ister'*, and I have no knowledge of you or a diplomatic exchange, I can only assume that you are, in fact, an intruder."

*Oz! Now would be the time...*

**Working on it. He just hailed security.**

The Zhyn looked at her menacingly. "So who are you, really?" he asked her again.

Molly's brain whirred.

*Oz, if this place goes into lockdown, can you still get me out?*

**I'm not sure. It's all in a different language, with different conjugations. I haven't had time to process what I need to in order to understand the building and security systems.**

*Are you saying 'it's all Greek'?*

**I'm saying it would be risky. Eventually I'd be able to figure it out; but you may end up being captured, in the meantime.**

*Okay. I'm all over it.*

Molly took a step back toward the door and felt a presence behind her. "Oh, there you are!" a familiar voice exclaimed.

Molly spun around to see Joel in a lab coat, next to the security guard who had accosted her earlier.

"This is her, then?" the guard asked.

Joel nodded. "Yes, and the boss wants to see her, pronto."

He turned to the big scientist named Els-ister. "Thanks for holding on to her for us. You know, we need more people who will ask the right questions to keep this facility secure. Thank you again."

And with that, he grabbed Molly by the arm, and hauled her out of the server room; whisking her off down the corridor, followed by the security guard.

The big guy, Els-ister, stood and watched them disappear as the door slid closed again.

He paused, staring at the door. Then he turned back to his colleague. "Okay, so the only problem with putting them into the stacked arrangement will be the amount of heat they generate. So we need to run some calculations on that…"

Molly trotted beside Joel as he strode decisively onward. She dared not utter a word, for fear of blowing their cover.

Joel had released her arm, and was looking straight ahead, still in character. The security guard was still following them, and at the next set of doors, Joel allowed him to lead the way. They followed him back through the wood-paneled foyer, and then toward the front door. The door slid open, allowing them out into the hazy daylight.

Joel turned to the guard. "Thank you for your help."

The guarded nodded, bowing slightly, and then turned on his heels to leave them be.

Molly waited until they were outside and several yards clear of the door. They were still walking in the direction of the rest of the base, rather than back to where they needed to go for the skylift.

She glanced up at Joel, whose pace had now slowed a little.

"That was close," she admitted.

"You're telling me!" he agreed.

Molly was still looking at him. "How the hell…?" she asked.

Joel smiled, relieved. "A bit of improvisation," he told her. "We need to clear the building; they still have cameras around the perimeter."

He pulled up his holo and pressed the quantum bead that was inserted into his wrist. "I'm just telling Jack that we're out and to meet us. She's found a hole in the fence, just over that way," he said, pointing off to the side of their current path.

Molly started walking in that direction. "Great. Let's get out of here."

Joel closed his holo and followed after her. "No arguments from me."

---

Jack was waiting by the fence. "Okay, soldiers, let's move," she whispered across to Molly and Joel as they approached.

The pair made their way through the fence, and followed Jack through the undergrowth and the cover of trees.

They found their way to the skylift and Joel pressed the call button. Molly kept a look out.

"I don't think we've been followed," she told the other two. "I'm just worried about the reaction once they find their weapons system has been deactivated."

*Oz, how long until deactivation?*

**Maybe five minutes.**

*Can you hold off on doing it immediately? I think we've more chance of getting away if they think that everything is as it should be.*

**Sure. Let me know when to go with it, then.**

*Okay.*

Molly turned to the others as they waited by the lift. "Oz is going to delay taking them offline… just until we're clear."

Jack nodded. "Great," she agreed, scanning the tree line around the skylift for early indications of company.

The lift arrived, and the three of them stepped in. Molly hit the button for orbit. "You know, I think we did well with this lift. It seems this is only for military use; the others are probably much closer to populated areas."

Joel nodded. "Yeah, the absence of advertising is also a clue!"

The three of them sniggered as the lift shot upwards, leaving their stomachs on the floor.

Molly steadied herself by grabbing the handrail, but Joel and Jack stood firm. The lift seemed to climb forever. Every time Molly thought they might have reached the top, it just kept going. She moved around a little, trying to resist her pacing habit.

"Wouldn't it be cool if there were windows in this thing?"

Joel leaned back against the wall. "Erm... No. I mean, you don't want to see how little material is holding this shaft in place."

Jack folded her arms. "Yeah, I'm with you, Joel. I just don't wanna know."

Molly leaned against the bar and held onto the handrail behind her.

*How's everything going down there, Oz? Anything we should know about?*

**Everything seems business as usual. The security guard is entering the incidents, but they won't be reviewed until later this evening.**

*Good.*

As the lift reached its lofty destination, it slowed to a halt. Molly felt a little dizzy by the change in movement. "Man, that was like a train ride in the wrong direction!" she commented.

Joel chuckled. "Yeah, that's a good way to explain it."

Jack was the first out onto the platform, and she immediately grabbed a rail and started looking around above them.

She pressed the quantum pearl on her wrist and talked into her holo. "Jack to Emma. Emma do you read?"

"Hello Jack," Emma responded immediately through her auditory implant. "I read you. What is your location, please?"

Jack glanced around, looking for the ship. "We're here on the platform. Top of the skylift. I can't see you."

"I'll be at your location in two minutes," Emma promised.

"Great," Jack acknowledged. "See you soon."

"Two minutes," Jack told the others. "Keep your eyes peeled."

For the next one minutes and thirty seconds, the three warriors stood looking up into orbit, watching all kinds of traffic drift past. There were satellite dishes, containers, and ships — from cargo ships through to smaller ones — all at different heights, carefully coordinated from the surface.

Their ride arrived, and the three of them grabbed onto the frame that Emma lowered through the hull of the ship.

As *The Empress* lifted up, gracefully clearing the hull of the skylift, the three were able to see down to the planet's surface, safely cocooned in the forcefield and the atmosphere of the ship.

Molly looked on in amazement. "Now that is a sight I'll never forget," she breathed, her voice full of awe.

"Yeah, I hear ya, sister," agreed Joel.

Jack was silent as she took it all in.

Moments later, the climbing frame started to retract, pulling them into the ship. They were greeted by a smiling Sean, who was standing over by Emma's console.

"Welcome back, motherfuckers," he beamed, his relief evident despite his casual manner. He moved over toward the frame to help them off of it as the hatch below them gently closed.

He grabbed Jack and then Molly. Joel had already dismounted, but the two hugged and slapped each other on the back anyway.

"Good to be back, man," Joel said.

"Yeah, glad you're safe, mate," Sean replied.

Jack and Molly looked at each other, grinning at the male bonding.

*Okay, Oz. We're clear. Wanna do your thing?*

**It would be my pleasure.**

"Sean?" Molly called over, interrupting Joel catching Sean up on the intricacies he had just been through. "Let's get us out of here and back to Gaitune, fast as we can."

Sean looked at her. "'Aye, boss!" he agreed, and headed out of the basement, back up to the cockpit.

Joel grinned at the two soldiers remaining. "Guess my retelling of rescuing your ass will have to wait till pizza time," he chuckled.

Molly smiled back at him. "Yeah. I guess so," she agreed. "But my thanking you doesn't." She walked over to Joel, carefully avoiding stepping on the hatch door — just in case — and threw her arms around his neck. "Thanks, Joel."

He hugged her and rubbed her back. "Any time," he said, glancing over at Jack watching them. He noticed that her expression was softer than he'd ever seen it. He dropped his eyes and whispered so only Molly could hear.

"Remember… I'm always coming for you."

Molly started to tear up, and nodded her head, still buried in Joel's embrace.

Joel could have sworn he felt a dampness on his neck. But when she pulled away, she turned around, and kept her back to him as she removed her gear and hung it on the racks. He couldn't tell if she'd been crying.

He glanced over at Jack, and spoke loudly so that Emma could still hear him on the intercom. "Okay, folks. Let's go debrief, and then get Molly down for her meditation session… else you *know* she'll be grumpy for the rest of the day."

Jack chuckled lightly.

Joel was pleased that the meditation was working for her, but he also felt her absence when she wasn't around. He watched her disappear through the door, and back to the main cabin.

# CHAPTER FIVE

**Planet Kurilia, Control Room of PrimeBase**

"Sir, something isn't right."

The commander on duty, Commander Thatle, spun around from his conversation, and moved back towards the console where the ensign was reporting from.

He peered over his shoulder to view the scanners. "What do you have, ensign?" he asked, briskly. He'd spent too much time monitoring this new operator, but he knew better than to dismiss anything out of hand.

"Sir," the ensign replied, "I believe there is something wrong with our scanners."

"Sir," said another voice behind him; a lieutenant was approaching. "I've just received a communication from security. It looks like our systems have been breached."

Just then, the emergency siren powered up in the control room. The lights flashed red and orange, warning of a breach.

The commander opened up a new panel with his handprint, and watched as the sit rep automatically unfolded in a hologram in front of him.

He felt the blood drain from his body as he read the code.

"It's a code 45," he said quietly.

The ensign looked up at his commander, and then at the lieutenant.

The lieutenant searched his memory. "That's a weapons attack... on our own systems?"

The commander nodded calmly. "That's right. We've been hacked. Our weapons are offline... meaning we're completely defenseless."

He turned to the next console and opened another program. He keyed in his access code before turning back to the lieutenant. "We need this planet on full alert. Close all airfields and all incoming traffic — skylifts and personnel movement. If our weapons have been knocked out, it's probably phase one of an attack. Switch communications to quantum-only."

The lieutenant saluted and the Commander nodded in response, dismissing him to carry out the orders. The lieutenant bustled away, and, a moment later, the quantum communicators of all staff in the control room were being loaded with the next battle instructions.

The commander walked briskly over to the space-monitoring station. "Have we incoming?" he asked quietly.

"No, sir," the operator responded. "Nothing out of the ordinary. Just the usual commercial traffic... Unless they're using jets that are smaller than we can detect now? Though chatter about the Etheric Empire would have reported that in a general briefing, so we'd know to expect that." The operator looked confused.

Commander Thatle wiped at his face with his hands and nodded. "Keep a careful eye out, and alert me the second you notice anything unusual."

The operator nodded. "Yes, sir."

*So much for a quiet shift,* he thought to himself.

He walked calmly back to his office to speak with the Lord

High Marshall. He would need authorization to scramble the space jets.

Back in his office, he sat down, neither rushing nor ambling. He could feel all three of his hearts beating fast, all out of sync. He felt nauseous, but his training had prepared him well for this moment. Remaining calm was the best way to maintain maximum cognitive function; and this is what always gave them the edge over the Leaths, the humans, and, well, practically every other race that cared to go into battle with them.

He opened up a quantum comm channel and waited for the Lord High Marshall to respond.

A minute later, the audio opened. "Yes?"

"Your Highness. This is Commander Thatle. I'm reporting a security breach. Our weapons have been taken offline. As yet, we have experienced no further attack, and our scanners haven't detected any incoming."

There was silence on the line. The audio timed out, so Commander Thatle couldn't even hear static or background noise. He waited and realized that he was holding his breath. He exhaled, counting the seconds before he should inhale again.

The waiting was excruciating.

Finally there was a noise on the line, and the audio channel reopened. "Scramble the jets, and assemble a reconnaissance team. The jets stay close; the reconnaissance should go out to the edge of our scanners to see if there is a problem with our detection. Keep me posted."

The commander nodded, even though the Lord High Marshall couldn't see him. "Yes, Your Highness," he confirmed.

The line fell silent, and Thatle closed the channel. Then he quietly began issuing the orders he'd been given.

**On board** *The Empress*

The team sat, perched, and stood in the cockpit.

Molly stood with her back to Sean and his console, so as not to pull his eye from what he needed to be doing.

"Okay, folks, this is just a quick update before we get back to base."

She brushed a strand of her dark hair out of her face. "The mission has been a success; Oz was able to take their weapons offline."

There was applause throughout the cockpit — Pieter even let out a 'whoop, whoop'. Joel looked at him as if to say *'Really?'* Pieter lowered his eyes and put his hand over his mouth, making the others chuckle.

Molly continued. "But, as you know, this is only part one of what we need to do. The next stage is to take out their bases completely — electricity, services, communications, and security — so they cannot build them up again easily."

She glanced around at the team, who was looking serious now. "Oz will know more about their systems in a matter of hours, and then we'll be able to design a plan. So when we get back to base, I recommend you getting a few hours' rack time while you can. Then we'll have a full team meeting down in the base conference room."

There were nods and grunts of acknowledgment all around.

Molly took a breath and clapped her hands. "Okay, folks. It's one hour back to base. Paige, come get me when we're on approach."

Paige nodded, and the audience broke up, talking and shuffling around. Molly headed back out to the lounge, followed by Joel, Paige, Jack, and Pieter. Brock stayed up front with Sean and Crash to talk more about the ship.

Molly didn't stop in the lounge. Instead, she headed back to the cargo area, leaving the chatter and activity behind.

As her eyes adjusted to the darkness, she found her way to her meditation shelf: a rack which would have been used to stack equipment and cargo. She hauled herself up and turned around to sit cross-legged on the mats and blankets she had accumulated there to make it a little more comfortable.

She placed the backs of her hands on her knees, closed her eyes, and drew her focus in to her breathing.

### Gaitune-67, Base conference room

Eight hours after landing back on Gaitune, the team rolled into the base conference room. Molly was looking peaceful, if not a little out of it.

"Looks like she's dosed up on the meditation," Joel joked to Paige.

Paige bit her lip. "Yeah. I wonder how long this is going to go on for? Or maybe this is it? She's going to have to do it forever..."

Their voices were hushed, and lost under the hum of the rest of the team talking, joking, and moving about the room.

Molly stood before them on the long, far side of the conference table.

"Okay, folks. Let's get into it," she said, starting the briefing.

Quiet fell over the room as the conversations ended, and attention was put on Molly.

"First off, great job on our first Etheric Empire mission. You should be pleased with yourselves; it was a huge success."

The team applauded briefly, and Molly could see the various team members exchanging glances and smiles, proud of their work.

Molly continued. "Oz has successfully connected into their systems, and, using Etheric tech, is able to monitor and download from their systems in real time. He and Pieter will be working to figure out how their systems operate, with a view for taking out the core areas."

She hit some buttons on her holo and it brought up two

screens in the center of the table. The first screen listed out their targets.

"We've got four key areas we have been tasked to take out: Power, communications, security, and weapons. We've already taken weapons offline, but without taking out the other three, they will soon be able to restore control of their weapons, and pose a threat both on and off world. Hence part two of this mission."

She looked around the room, making sure she wasn't moving too fast. Then she flicked to the second screen, which was a three dimensional, layered map, showing the different networks they knew of.

"What you see on the second screen," she continued, "is an approximation of their security networks, their data centers, their power grids and generators, as well as their communication hubs and artillery."

Pieter looked at the screen, squinting a little to try and determine all the detail. The others just watched their task unfold.

Molly straightened up a little. "There's one other thing you need to know at this point," Molly added. "We have strict instructions to minimize all casualties, and to leave civilian systems unaffected.

Pieter slouched back in his seat. "There goes my idea of using an EMP to take out the main nodes for all services."

Molly looked over at him. "Yes, that would have been a good idea. Except that their sensitive areas are all protected by EMP-proof casing. It wouldn't work."

Pieter looked both surprised and intrigued. Before he could speak, Molly put her hand up. "I'll show you how that works later. But for now, it's safe to assume it's not an option."

Joel shifted forward in his seat and raised his hand a little to get Molly's attention. Molly turned to face him, directly opposite her on the other side of the conference table. Joel put his hand down. "Molly, why has the Empire decided to do such a precision exercise? I thought they were all about bitch slapping the enemy down when they needed it?"

Sean had been looking at Joel, his hands clasped on the table in front of him. When he heard Joel's description of the Empire, he put his head down so no one could see his face; but almost everyone noticed his shoulders shaking silently as he laughed.

Molly looked thoughtful for a moment.

"Well," she began, "part of it is because the General is under pressure to reduce the military capabilities of the Empire. Bitch-slapping potential allies is probably the fastest way to have that enforced. He has to go along with some of it for now, for the sake of maintaining certain alliances. But, at the same time, some of those so-called alliances are… well, I guess the word is 'conspiring…' against the Empire to attack them at a later date. This is just one way of reducing the number of allies our opposition can call upon when the shit hits the fan. The other thing is, this can't be traced back to the General. No matter what."

Molly paused, trying to decide whether to share the other details. She shrugged, making her decision to tell them.

"Plus," she admitted, "I kinda have a problem with needlessly killing people. I've convinced the General to give us an opportunity to see if we can make this more effective, and less bloody. If we can use all our tech, intel, and smarts to take out just their military capabilities, and leave everyone alive, then I think this will set a new standard in the rules of engagement. I think we can raise the bar on how wars are fought and how politics are handled, and hopefully set an example for how individual civilizations should treat their own citizens."

She smiled sheepishly. "Of course, if this all goes horribly wrong, I'll be eating humble pie — and no doubt our Empress will hear about it, and give me no end of shit for ages to come…"

The team chuckled and sniggered. Paige shifted in her seat, leaning forward over the table a little. "I think it's an excellent idea. I mean, if the Etheric Empire can fight a war without spilling a drop of blood, we'll command the respect of those who are aspiring to do better in their efforts."

Sean snorted. "Yeah, and inspire confusion in those battle-hungry warlords."

Molly pulled her lips to one side of her face. "Yeah. I'm not sure how this would go down against the 'iron fist' attitude, but I suppose that will become apparent once this new way of doing things becomes established." She took a deep breath. "*If* it becomes established," she clarified. "We just need to get this first one right."

She glanced around, and her eyes fell on Pieter.

"Besides, in principle, the more we know about our enemies, the more effective we can be; not just in defeating them, but in brokering peace and relationships down the line. I'd much rather have the Zhyn as an ally for the next decade, than have their planet be a post-apocalyptic mess of nuclear disaster, and a hell-hole on which only the most vicious people can survive."

The team went quiet, contemplating the two alternatives. Sean's head was down again, but this time his shoulders weren't shaking, Molly noticed. He was perhaps the only one who would have known what went on back on her planet of origin in the last hundred years or so.

She took a moment to gather her thoughts, and then pulled up a third holoscreen in the center of the table.

"Okay, here are our areas of responsibility," she announced. "Power. What we know is that each base has its own generators, a connection to a military grid, and their own backup generators. The backup generators can go for several weeks, but they aren't capable of meeting all the base's power needs; just their emergency needs."

The power grid was illuminated on the map as she talked about it. "There are vulnerable areas… but each of these will need to be affected at once, if we are to be successful. This may require boots on the ground."

She glanced over at Sean, Jack, and Joel, who sat next to each other, in front of Molly and slightly to the right.

"So, to overcome not being able to use EMPs, we've been considering the option of some kind of quantum pulse that will overload this and their data systems. Brock, can you get with Pieter, Oz, and ADAM, if needs be, and see if we can build something that will take out all these capabilities?"

Brock's eyes were wide, and Molly could see him visibly recoil. "I… I… I don't know if that is even possible."

Molly smiled. "Brock, you are the most capable engineer I've ever known. Plus, you have the tech of the Etheric Empire at your fingertips. You can re-engineer anything you need in order to do this. I believe in you."

Brock looked flustered. "Well, er. I suppose I ought to give it a go, then…"

The group chuckled. Pieter was sitting next to Brock, and slapped him gently on the back, giving him a wink. Paige smiled at him from across the table.

"Good," Molly confirmed. "Just let me know some idea of time scales by tomorrow."

Brock nodded, making notes on his holo.

Molly flicked her holo, and the next word appeared on screen number three. "Comms!" she called out. "Maya, Paige…" she looked over at the pair sitting together. "I want you to study the social dynamics of how they are structured — their hierarchy, their ways. If we're going to beat them, we need to know more about them. Oz can download transcripts of conversations, and anything else you need off their systems."

Paige and Maya both nodded, taking notes on their holos, and conferring quietly with each other.

"Security," Molly announced the next area. "Oz, if you could, finish up on whatever you need to learn for their language and programming structure. Then we need to look deeper into taking down all their security protocols."

Oz's audio clicked on over the conference room feed. "I believe that the Empire already has some insight — into their language, at least. ADAM has agreed to share that download, which will save a lot of time. I can figure out the rest from context."

Molly nodded, listening. "Great, make it so. And lean on Pieter for any creative leaps; he's a resource, in that regard."

Most of the members around the table glanced over at Pieter, who blushed a deep red. Brock comically returned the slap on the back.

"Dude, you got this," he told him, mimicking Pieter's voice, accent, and intonation.

There were more than a few laughs around the table.

Molly brought up the final word on the slide. "Training," she told them. She glanced over at Sean.

"Sean, if you would, we need Jack, Joel, and myself trained up on the rest of the toys in the armory. Something tells me that this isn't the first time the Empire has had to head down to the surface of this, or any, planet. We need all the tech advantages we can muster."

Sean nodded.

Molly continued. "But Crash could also do with your input..."

Sean nodded again. "Not a problem. I can do my Freddy Kruger impersonation..."

Molly looked confused. Pieter piped up to fill her in. "It's an Earth reference. Everywhere you turn, there he is..."

Molly smiled. "Ohhhhh," she said, still not really understanding the reference. She turned to Crash, still smiling a little. "And that leaves Crash."

Crash looked up at her, a faint smile on his lips, barely detectable.

"Crash," she finished, "I'd like you to get in as many sim hours as possible." Her face dropped and became serious. "But make sure you take proper breaks and rest time. I'm not having you burning yourself out so you're good for nothing when we have to fly."

Crash nodded solemnly. "Yes, ma'am," he said, before allowing a smile to return to his face. "I can do me the flying," he added with a twinkle in his eye.

# CHAPTER SIX

**Planet Kurilia, Koin Star System, Zhyn Empire**

Shaa paced the width of his enormous office, a few feet from the paneled windows. "This has that human, Reynolds, written all over it," he growled, his breath catching short in his lungs.

He was getting old, and his body was starting to feel it. Being stuck behind a desk and unable to fight anymore wasn't helping his health, or his temperament.

Davon watched his master as he stood a short distance back from the desk — his usual spot for addressing His Highness. He shuffled his feet awkwardly, biding his time for the moment to reel the conversation in a useful direction.

"Find me evidence it was Reynolds!" Shaa commanded.

Davon didn't move. Shaa kept pacing. A few strides later, he turned and looked at Davon. "What is it?" he snapped, his bluster forgotten, and now concerned for what other news he had to deal with.

Davon rubbed his hands a little, trying to soothe himself while minimizing his fidgeting. "Your Highness, we have already begun gathering intel," he began. He took a deeper breath before continuing. "It seems the attack was on our computer systems only. There is still no evidence of a full invasion."

Shaa turned and walked back towards the desk and rested his hands on the back of his antigrav chair. "And?" he asked, more curious than demanding now.

Davon continued. "It seems we had an intruder breach our data center not an hour prior." He paused, waiting to see if Shaa would explode.

Shaa remained silent — too silent for Davon's liking. Davon continued. "It seems two humans managed to access the data center, and plant some kind of code. It was in our new language... which rules out the Etheric Empire. They only had access to our old code, which we've also been using as a diversion..." His voice trailed off as he watched Shaa's reaction.

The blue Zhyn went a deep red, and then turned purple around the boney frill framing his head. Still he remained silent. Seething. He gripped the chair and pulled it out roughly from behind his desk and sat down. There he sat for several moments, waves of anger pouring off him, as he fought to compose himself.

Davon waited patiently, relieved that the windows were at least still intact. Hell, relieved that *he* was still intact.

Shaa eventually seemed to have released the majority of his fury. He looked up at Davon, anger still smoldering in his eyes. "But if they were humans, surely they won't have been acting alone?"

Davon shook his head. "At this stage, we don't know. Although," he paused, wondering whether to broach the next thought. "It's not the Etheric Empire's style. We know Reynolds would try and broker a negotiation. If he wanted us disarmed, he would have at least suggested it as part of the terms of *his* disarmament. The Empress of the Etheric Empire would have come in here with incendiaries, and blown us all to shit. This group - whoever they are - just don't seem to fit with either of those approaches. And there is still no indication the Federation knows anything about these secret bases."

Shaa shook his head. "And it begs the question, how did they get hold of our code to be able to even read our data, let alone hack through our security?" He leaned his arms on his desk and hung his head a little. "Humans aren't capable of reading our language. The code is too sophisticated; we checked that already. They just don't have the working memory…"

"…So they couldn't have been acting alone." Davon finished his sentence for him.

Shaa nodded, his eyes now solemn more than enraged. "And that," he added, "brings us on to which of our allies have we shared our developments with, who could potentially do this?"

Davon bowed his head respectfully. "I shall find out straight away, Your Highness."

Shaa waved his hand to dismiss him. "Conduct your investigation quietly, though. We don't want anything getting out, if it is one of our allies that we have to strike down."

Davon bowed again, and then left the room. Shaa's gaze followed him out, before dropping to the desk in front of him.


**Gaitune-67, Safe house, Common area**

Molly finished reviewing the document and looked up from her holo. Paige had been tracking her eye movement, trying to deduce her opinions from her facial expressions. Finally she was going to hear Molly's take on her editorial.

Paige looked at Molly expectantly. "So? What do you think?" she asked, her eyes hopeful.

The three girls were sitting on the sofas, while the hub of the others buzzed around them. Sean and Joel were watching the holo screen, which was playing some kind of sport that ADAM had recommended. They had the sound routed through their implants.

Molly glanced at Maya, who was still engrossed in reading the article. She looked briefly down at her holo again. "I think it's great."

Paige smiled. "Really?" she asked brightly.

Molly nodded. "Yeah, it's interesting. It's got good pace."

Paige detected there was something Molly was holding back on. "But…?" she pressed.

Molly frowned a little and scrolled back up. "I'm just thinking about how a reader would perceive it. It might need a stronger hook at the beginning. Maybe think of what it takes to attract someone's attention so that they know there is a reason, a benefit to them, to keep reading."

Paige pursed her lips and looked down at her copy. She scribbled a few notes. "So, from a customer's perspective, you mean?"

Molly nodded. "Yeah, that's right. Imagine your ideal customer is looking at the article, and then tell them up front the thing that would most get their attention."

Paige nodded. "Okay, great. I'll have to think about that."

Maya lifted her head, and Paige turned to her next. "Well?" Paige asked.

Maya bobbed her head. "It's great. I agree with Molly. But how do they get the product?"

Paige slumped back in her chair. "I'm still looking at manufacturing options. Looks like it's going to have to happen on Ogg, for cost reasons."

Molly looked at her, impressed with her progress. She closed her holo. "You've got a quote in?"

Paige nodded. "Yeah. I like a couple of companies in the inner system, but there's one on Ogg that I think is going to be able to handle the process, *and* is going to be the cheapest."

Molly smiled. "Well, that's good, then."

Paige looked a little anxious. "Well, I hope so. It's a big step."

Molly smiled. "You can do this," she told Paige, looking deep into her eyes until Paige nodded.

Molly turned to Maya. "So, you were thinking about a call to action at the end of the piece?"

Maya nodded, pulling up her screen again. "Yeah. I think that it would be stronger if we deliberately led people into what their next action is. That's how you capitalize on this kind of thing. It need only be a single line: 'if you want to try this new, bulletproof nail color, then click here.' Boom. And you're done."

Paige frantically took down the notes as Maya talked. She was silent for a few more seconds. "Okay. I've got it," she told them. "Thanks so much for your help... I'll go get those other bits sorted, and let your friend at Newstainment know what's happening."

Maya smiled, closing her holo. "Great stuff. It's going to be a hit. You're doing great!"

Paige smiled weakly. "Thanks. I appreciate your support," she said, looking first at Maya and then at Molly.

Molly smiled and stood up. "Any time," she said. "Now I need to go check on some work that Oz is sending through," she added, excusing herself from the group.

As she walked past where Paige and Maya were sitting, she started to feel a little lightheaded.

Paige was the first to recognize what was going on, and turned in her seat to see what was happening.

Molly kept walking, moving off into the center of the common area, and then to the foyer. With each step, she felt a little fainter.

A little stranger.

She spotted Neechie just to her right. Brock was coming towards the common area from the basement door. He said something to her, but she couldn't hear it. She could only see his lips moving.

The world around her went blue, flashing her into another world. She recognized what was happening.

She felt hands on her arms from people behind her grabbing hold to steady her as she wavered.

The blue world had people in it, too. There were military people walking around; none of them seemed to see her. Neechie was still there, though.

Then the world flashed back to normal. She gazed at the Sphinx, noticing he had been in both places. She felt hot and faint and sick…

The world flashed again, into another blue place where everything was rock.

She was completely alone.

It looked like Gaitune - but there was nothing around. No landmarks. Nothing she recognized.

Then she looked up, and there was an enormous ship hovering above her. It was large and menacing, yet she felt safe and protected; as if she were somehow distanced from what was happening.

Suddenly, she flashed back to the real world, and her vision started to go black at the edges.

She was aware of falling and hitting something with a *thump*, but nothing in her body hurt. She was enveloped in comfort, and then nothing.

### Gaitune-67, Safe house, Molly's quarters

Molly slowly became aware of feeling comfort, like she was wrapped in cotton, and completely at ease. And then she became aware of her body.

"She's waking up, Joel." It was Paige's voice. Molly stirred, opening her eyes, and looked over to where the sound was coming from, as her eyes adjusted to the light.

Paige was smiling down at her. Molly heard the scrape of a chair and movement, and then Joel appeared behind Paige.

Molly tried to bring herself around quicker. "What

happened?" she asked, trying to use her voice – which felt like it hadn't been used in a month.

Joel answered first. "You took a tumble," he told her. "How you feeling?"

Molly tried to shrug from her lying down position in the bed. "I dunno. I just woke up from a nap."

Paige interjected. "You didn't just fall. You jumped realms again. Do you remember what happened?" she asked.

Molly felt confused. Her mind was foggy as she clung to the sensation of comfort that was fast evaporating. She searched her memory like a dream that was fading away. "I remember something. I remember being out on the rock... Out there... I remember military people walking around this place..."

Paige looked across at Joel. "What if... I know this sounds crazy, but she might have been time jumping. There were probably military people here, once. Before the base was abandoned."

Joel nodded. Paige reached forward to Molly's neck. Molly flinched, afraid that what she was about to do would tickle her. Paige fumbled a second for her necklace. "Looks like this isn't helping."

Molly rolled onto her side, and hauled herself into a sitting position. "It had been about five hours since I meditated..." she offered.

Paige frowned. "We need to find a more permanent solution. Something tells me this isn't just going to disappear..."

Molly sighed, hanging her head.

Paige looked at her, still frowning, her eyes filled with concern. "Can I get you anything? A mocha, perhaps?"

Molly shook her head. "No thanks," she said quietly. "It's still making me feel nauseous."

That's when she realized Sean was in the room. He stood up from his seat in her living room, and wandered over to the bed, on the other side from Paige and Joel. "That's something we need to look into," he said seriously. "The nanocytes make it so that there isn't anything physically wrong with you. There can't be. That's their job... to fix anything that is broken, and make everything inside balanced." He looked solemn as he glanced across at Joel. "I think there is something else going on," he explained.

Molly stuck out her bottom lip. "I hate this."

Paige rubbed her arm. "I know, honey. We'll figure it out, though. Just you hang in there."

Molly started to peel back the blankets that Paige had covered her over with while she slept. "How long was I out for?" she asked.

Paige checked her holo. "About half an hour. Maybe a little more."

Molly nodded as she got up. Joel and Paige backed up to give her space.

"What are you doing?" Paige asked.

Molly stretched a little, finding her house shoes. "I'm going to go have a word with ADAM, and see if we can't get this fixed once and for all. I can't keep going through this, *and* run a base. Or show up on an op. It's in the Empire's interest to help us solve this..."

There were nods and sounds of agreement from the others. Molly found her hoodie on the end of the bed, and pulled it on as she ambled gingerly out of the room.

Joel watched her go, shaking his head.

Paige looked up at him. "I'm really worried about her. What if she came back wrong?"

Sean had been heading towards the door, but when he heard Paige's comment, he turned around with passion in his eyes. "Don't ever say that again. She's just adjusting. We're going to figure this out." He hit the panel on the door, and disappeared out into the corridor after Molly.

# CHAPTER SEVEN

**Gaitune-67, Base, Ops Room**

Molly arrived in the Ops Room, having agreed to let Sean accompany her in case she fell and experienced head trauma. Now, perched at her usual console, she sat awaiting ADAM's arrival.

Sean sat a few consoles back, in an antigrav chair, carefully watching his leader: she was swinging her legs, her hands shoved into her hoodie pockets, with her hood up, covering her hair.

It took a few minutes, but ADAM arrived. "Greetings, Molly. How goes it?" he asked.

Molly straightened up a little, pulling herself back from her idle thoughts. "Hi, ADAM. I was wondering if we could get some help on these episodes I've been having? The meditations have only helped so much, and Paige's pendant helped a little, but it feels like we're fighting an incoming tide."

She paused. "Did you speak with your contact about helping me? The classified one?"

ADAM's audio clicked on again. "I did indeed, and she agreed to help. She's just wrapping up some other things for us right now, but she should be available soon. I will have her reach out to you as soon as she is able."

Sean watched. He could see Molly's face light up in relief.

"That's great!" she exclaimed brightly. "Who is she? And how will she contact me?"

ADAM's voice was serious again. "As it happens, it's someone you've already met. She'll swing by when she can; I have no doubt. In the meantime, keep up with the meditation practice. She has assured me that it is the most effective thing you can do until she can get to you."

Molly eyed the console suspiciously. "Who is she, though?"

ADAM chuckled a little. "Ah, I like it when you get surprises, so I'm not going to tell you."

Molly scowled a little. "Dammit, ADAM. This is serious! It's no time for games. Just tell me!"

ADAM seemed to be smiling as he responded. "Molly, I'm a very old AI; there isn't much left in this world that gives me pleasure. But surprising you and giving Sean shit are two of my favorite pleasures. Don't deny an old man that."

Molly mumbled something inaudibly under her breath.

"No need to be like that, Ms. Bates," ADAM continued. "It's good for you not to always have all the answers."

Molly scowled at the console, wishing that ADAM was more embodied so she could hit him. "Yeah, well, if I die, or end up in some hell dimension, I want it written on my tombstone: 'Here lies Molly Bates. Dead because some jackass of an AI wanted to get his ya-yas in at her expense.'"

ADAM chuckled again. "Ms. Bates, that is something I can certainly arrange for you."

Molly started slipping down from the invisible stool she had perched herself on. "Fine," she told him.

"Well, okay, then. Your person will be in touch soon. Good luck, Ms. Bates."

"Thanks, ADAM. Bye for now…" she said. The audio channel clicked off again.

Sean stood up and ambled over. "Well, sounds like some progress was made, at least."

Molly shook her head. "That guy… honestly. I swear he and Oz are more human than most of the humans I know."

Sean rolled his eyes. "I know. Tell me about it. The guy has been jerking my chain for…"

Molly glanced up at him waiting to hear how many years he had known ADAM.

Sean caught himself just in time. "… for ancestors know how long," he concluded, grinning.

Molly shook her head, and headed out of the ops room. Finding out Sean's actual age wasn't high on the list of tasks requiring her energy right now.

She paused, turning back to him and narrowing her eyes. "And I swear Oz is becoming a bad influence on him. Didn't ADAM used to be more stuck-up, before he and Oz started mind-melding?"

Sean shrugged as he followed her out. "You know, you may have a point there."

### Gaitune-67, Basement, Workshop

Pieter and Brock sat at one of the benches in the workshop. Crash had wandered in earlier, on a break from the flight simulator; but hearing that they were deep in technical discussions, had grabbed his antigrav mug and disappeared again.

Brock sighed. "I think Molly is right about something needing to be quantum," he admitted.

Pieter nodded while typing something on his holo. "Yeah. That will help with putting the charges in the different areas. I wonder if we can trigger an entangled nuclear reaction…" he mused, his eyes lighting up quietly at the thought of the engineering to do that.

Brock shook his head. "Nah ha. We only want to take out these specific targets. Nothing else; no fallout. That takes nukes out of the equation. But..." He pulled up another screen and shared it with Pieter. "I'm wondering... Oz? Do we know the composition of those EMP-proof walls?"

Oz spoke to them over the local inter comm audio. "We do. Just one moment." A second later, the wall schematics and materials used flew up onto the shared screens.

Brock dragged his finger inside the schematic, pulling apart the construction. "Okay; it looks like mostly steel and concrete lined with a metal frame, which forms a Faraday cage. That's the protection."

He glanced up at Pieter, seeing if Pieter shared his excitement. Pieter waved his hand casually. "Yeah, but that kind of material we could blow out with a normal explosive."

Brock grinned. "Exactly. So the problem has moved from being how do we blow up the generators using some quantum explosion tech that hasn't been invented yet, to how do we blast through the Faraday cages, by *triggering* the explosions quantumly?"

Pieter grinned. "That's brilliant!" he exclaimed.

Brock shrugged. "No, brilliant would have been inventing a new way of blowing shit up. But this? This might just solve our problem."

Pieter frowned. "So the detonation could be done with a normal radio pulse, then?"

Brock shook his head. "I don't think so. I think these guys have been smart about the way they've arranged their assets. There is no one point where you could set a radio signal, and have it take out all the cages at once. In fact..." he said, pulling up the map and zooming in a little... "If these guys are as smart as I think they are, I wouldn't put it past them to have some kind of radio jamming, or to have cages built all over the place, to protect their systems."

Pieter shook his head. "Wow, the things you need to be aware of when people are likely to come get you."

Brock looked up at him. "Yeah, I know. Scary, eh?" He glanced around the workshop. "I'll bet this place was built with all that kinda shit taken into account, too. I mean... why else would they put us on a frikkin' asteroid?"

Pieter grinned. "Right. It ain't for the scenery... or the great pizza!"

Brock put his fist out to bump Pieter's. "Word!" he said before returning to the task at hand. "I don't believe the Etheric Empire has designed anything quite like that before," he added seriously.

Pieter brightened a little, his inner inventor hoping he could come out to play. "So we'd be designing it from scratch?" he clarified.

Brock stood up and scratched the back of his head. "Possibly." He swung his hips a little, and then stretched out his back. "Let me run through our artillery list." He pulled up another screen. "Okay. Here we are. We have quantum comms, quantum blasters - but all they seem to do is vaporize whatever they fire at..." He kept reading down the list with his eyes.

Pieter had drifted off into his own thoughts, no longer listening. "You know," he mused, "I'm wondering if the comm devices can be used. They just need to receive a signal, and then that signal can trigger the detonation."

Brock straightened up and closed his screen. "You're right! Lemme go and grab a couple more from the store, and see if we can crack them open enough to rewire them." He grinned broadly, the excitement of tinkering with tech welling up in him.

Oz chipped in. "Good thinking. I'll see if I can find some schematics."

Brock waltzed out of the workshop via the demon door. Oz

disappeared from the audio feed to access the extensive records ADAM had interfaced him with for the base.

Pieter sat on his own, wondering what he should do. "Right then," he said to the empty workshop. "I'm going to go get a soda," he announced, standing up from his workspace and heading into the safe house. He was pleased his idea had moved things on, but his inner child did not like being left alone.

### Gaitune-67, Base, Artillery warehouse

Molly and Joel watched Sean pulling gear off the racks down one of the aisles. Jack had her arms folded as she wandered over to where they were standing. She stood and watched the activity for a moment, then turned to Molly. "You sure you're up to this?" she asked quietly. Her face seemed to be one of genuine concern.

Molly was a little taken aback. "Er. Yeah," she answered, smiling appropriately.

Jack shoved her hands in her pockets, recognizing Molly's discomfort with the social interaction, and took half a step back. She turned away, putting her attention on Sean, but not letting the conversation drop. "You know, it's okay not to be okay," Jack told her. Her voice was gentle, but matter-of-fact.

Joel pretended he was engrossed with checking out the machinery Sean was fussing with.

Molly folded her arms too, mirroring Jack subconsciously. "Yeah. I'm okay," she said taking a deep breath. "I'll probably go hit the meditation in half an hour, though."

Jack bobbed her head. "Okay. But remember, in order for this team to be operational, *you* need to be functioning."

Molly smiled, and looked Jack in the eye. "Is that C.O. Nolan speaking?" she asked, a short smile playing on her lips.

Jack grinned her enigmatic smile that lit up her whole face. "You *know* it is," she responded playfully.

Molly couldn't help but brighten up. It was just one of those moments that reminded her how thankful she was to have such a great team of people around her. She flushed with gratitude, despite feeling a little out of sorts.

Sean, meanwhile, had mounted a piece of gear over one shoulder, holding it with his right hand. In the other hand, he carried a black sack that hung down by his legs. He dropped both in front of him, once he was out in the open and clear of the shelving.

Joel regarded the gear on the floor. "So, what've we got?" he asked, a glimmer of anticipation in his eyes.

Sean reached down to the weapon he had carried over, and picked it up as one would a gun. Various pieces unfolded and locked into place spontaneously as he did so. It was as if the four-foot-long weapon knew it was going to be used.

Joel's mouth dropped open. Jack gasped, her face lit with delight. Even Molly smiled, impressed.

Sean grinned his dirty grin, like he'd just scored. "Yeah, baby. You know what I like!" he exclaimed, enjoying the team's reaction, as well as the feel of the weapon in his hands.

The machinery had extended itself over his shoulder, and curled over his back. It had also clamped around his arm, so that Sean was almost cradling it.

Molly walked around him to get a better look at what had just happened. "Hard to tell if you're holding the gun, or if it's holding you!" she remarked.

Joel chuckled. "That's what you get when you're half-cyborg!" he retorted, his eyes twinkling, waiting for a reaction from Sean.

Sean narrowed his eyes and pointed the weapon in Joel's general direction. Joel put his hands up in mock surrender. "Dude, just sayin'!" he exclaimed.

Jack shook her head, smiling at them goofing around. "So come on, what does it do?" she pressed, getting them back on task.

Sean switched into trainer mode. "What you're looking at is

the Barrier Blaster. Out there," he explained, "waving his arm in the direction of the hangar deck, you're going to encounter races that can't be dropped with a normal gun. For instance, the Zhyn, who you met yesterday," he said, looking at Joel and Molly. "Their skin is too thick for normal stun guns and bullets."

He shifted the weapon in his arms, readjusting his position, and flipped a switch. The weapon powered up with a gentle hum. Sean's face relaxed, as if he was comforted to have the weapon activated and back in his arms again.

Jack frowned a little. "Why is it called the 'Barrier Blaster'?" she asked.

Sean shrugged. "Well, it can also be used to take down barriers — like forcefields. Rips a hole right through them, and then when the integrity of the field is compromised, the whole thing collapses. Plus," he added, "it wouldn't be politically prudent to call them 'Zhyn-Blasters'; especially if we end up welcoming them and their troops into the Federation."

Jack clamped a hand over her mouth to hide that she was smiling. Sean chuckled a little. "Can you imagine doing this training, and explaining that in front of a class of humans, Estarians, and a few Zhyn? Baaaad idea."

Joel laughed too. "I suppose that was the General's foresight coming into play!"

Sean bobbed his head in agreement. "Yeah, maybe. Though there are some pretty smart people working on this gear. This was probably the brainchild of Jean Dukes."

Molly noted the name, repeating it in her head a few times.

**Why so important to remember?**

*Sean is still a bit withholding when it comes to explaining everything going on in the Empire. I figure that the more points of reference we have, the more chance we have of learning the ropes. Besides, if we need mods made, who better to ask than the inventor?*

**I see your point.**

Joel grinned, enjoying the process of learning about the new gear. He glanced over at Molly to smile at her, but noticed she was looking thoughtful. "What is it?" he asked.

Molly tilted her head a little and rolled her lips inward. "I dunno. It's a little…" She hesitated.

Joel stepped closer, allowing Jack and Sean to continue talking about the machinery. "What?" he asked, looking concerned now.

Molly glanced up at him briefly, before hugging her arms tighter and looking at the floor. She took a deep breath. "Well, what I'm about to say isn't going to sound very military of me."

Joel eyed her carefully. "But?" he pressed.

Molly shrugged. "Why with all the killing?" She looked up, trying to waylay the protest she knew would be coming from the space marine's mouth. "I know, sometimes it's necessary; but it just seems so superfluous a lot of the time. In fact, I'm starting to really wonder if it's the most efficient way to maintain peace and allow the Empire to thrive."

Joel had closed his mouth and was listening intently. Molly shook her head, and held her hand up to shield her face from him a little. "I mean, I know that military might has its place — but what if we could achieve our objectives without all the violence? We're talking about stopping peoples' hearts, like it's a computer game. But it's not. It's real. And if we can be in and out of an op by just disabling people for the duration, isn't that the smarter play?"

Sean and Jack caught the tail end of the conversation, and their mood sobered slightly.

Molly noticed that all the attention was now on her.

She dropped her arms to her sides. "Okay, we need to learn how this kit works, so let's keep going. But I'm going to think about how we can get some of this adapted so that it is more humane for those instances when we don't have to just blow the fuck out of people."

The others just stared at her. Molly couldn't read them, though.

"Look," she continued, "I know this isn't what you want to hear, but I have to at least consider other options." She looked from face to face to face hoping to see a hint they understood.

Molly turned to leave. Joel reached out to her and grabbed her elbow. She turned back to him, ready to argue, but his face was serious, and she could tell there was emotion behind his eyes.

"You're right," he said softly. "Know that while this," he waved between Jack, Sean and himself. "Seems like kids in a candy store when we get excited about blowing shit up. We *know* what it means to take a life. Only the seriously fucked up enjoy killing."

Molly shook her head a little, trying to understand what he had just said.

"We all know," he repeated again. This time a little louder, his voice cracking. He looked back at Jack and Sean. "I mean, look at what has happened throughout history when people have grown in military capabilities and gotten more and more efficient at killing each other. It breeds fear; and fear breeds anger, and more armament. Along with a drive to find uglier and bigger ways to kill others."

He turned back to Molly.

"If there is a way to do what needs to be done without inciting fear and hatred and killing?" His eyes had begun to fill with understanding. "Then we are behind you 100%".

Sean lowered the weapon he was holding. It seemed to be controlled by his intention somehow, because it retracted and folded itself away back to its original configuration. Sean looked down at it thoughtfully. He rubbed his free hand over his face before looking up at Molly.

"You know," Sean said seriously, "the *worst* part of this job is knowing that you've taken another person's life. That stays with you. Forever. And the longer you do it, the more blood you have on your hands."

He looked up at Molly, and then the others. "And you tell yourself it's necessary. And you pretend like it doesn't bother you, and that it's just a job. But…" his voice trailed off.

Jack moved her gaze from Sean back to Molly. She nodded her head. "I'm in, too. If we can be safe, and not have to kill people, we have a duty *not* to."

Molly felt overwhelmed. This was meant to be a run-of-the-mill training session; not a complete change in their ethos. She felt a weight of responsibility hit her.

*What if it isn't possible? What if I am putting my people in danger? But then, what if it* is *possible? To not be the cause of so much violence? And with them all in agreement, figuring it out and implementing it will be so much easier.*

In that moment, she felt so validated it made her feel strong. Looking at her team, 100% with her on her maverick idea, her heart actually hurt. She took a deep breath, moving the energy through her chest.

She felt her voice catch in her throat. "Okay. Great. For now, I'll let you continue the training. I need to go meditate, but we can pick this idea up later."

She excused herself, feeling a little uncomfortable with the strange mixture of emotions as she hurried toward the door and out of sight.

# CHAPTER EIGHT

**Gaitune-67, Base, Hangar Deck, On board *The Empress***

"So how come you call yourself 'Emma,' when the ship is called *'The Empress'*?"

Emma's voice rang through the cockpit. "I thought it would be disrespectful to call myself 'the Empress'."

Crash didn't dare take his eyes from his instruments. "Because that's Bethany Anne's title?"

"Correct," Emma agreed.

"Hmm," Crash mused, as his grip tightened on the joystick. "I hadn't thought of that. I just read in the training preliminaries that the convention was that the EI took the name of the ship."

Crash pulled up a little, carefully avoiding a simulated oncoming magneto cloud.

"A little more," Emma coaxed.

Crash thought for a second, checking that he wasn't going to inadvertently knock another parameter off-kilter by resuming the tilt upwards. He decided he was probably okay, and continued with the maneuver.

"You've got it." Emma told him.

Crash exhaled quietly as his eyes scanned both the simulation holo in front of him, and all the instruments he'd been checking on and off for the last several hours.

His brain was becoming fatigued, but the intermittent serotonin hits he was generating every time he got something right, or touched into that bliss he felt when he was flying, kept him from taking a break.

Some of the instruments started detecting a gravitational pull. He scanned the other instruments and then the map, looking for what might be causing it. He looked up on the screen that gave him an advanced visual across the EM-spectrum.

Nothing.

"Er... Emma?" he asked, his voice slightly hesitant.

"Yes, Crash?" she responded.

Crash's normally blank expression portrayed a rare look of concern. "I'm having problems with this one. No radiation spikes. No visuals. But we're detecting a gravitational pull."

Emma's voice was calm and collected. "Okay, so what's the first thing you should do?"

Crash checked his instruments again. "Drop out of warp?" he ventured.

"Yes," Emma agreed.

Crash made the adjustments and dropped the simulation out of warp.

"Then what?" she prompted.

Crash searched his mind for the correct sequence. "Check instruments, scanners, the map, and then visuals."

Emma was silent, as he ran through his routine.

"Okay, all clear," Crash reported, still puzzled.

Emma entered into teaching mode. "So you have a g-field detected, but nothing else. What could possibly be causing that?" she prompted again.

Crash rolled his lips inward, and then took a deep breath. "A black hole!" he said, his tone suddenly brighter.

Emma remained quiet for a moment. Crash could feel her

rolling her EI eyes behind the console. "A black hole," she explained, "would be emitting energy from its event horizon. We'd have a whisper. Or we'd see light distortions."

Crash scanned the visual, searching for his theory to be correct. He shook his head as he scanned. "Nope," he reported back.

"Okay, think of it this way," Emma said slowly. "What emits radiation in a very narrow plain, making it impossible to detect from certain angles?"

Crash tried to slap his forehead, but then remembered he needed to keep his hands on the controls. "Pulsar!" he exclaimed.

"Right!" agreed Emma. "And you're welcome."

"What for?" Crash asked, suddenly confused again.

Emma's voice was lighter now. "For saving your life, and the lives of your whole team aboard this mission."

Crash shook his head, chuckling. "How come you have a sense of humor?" he asked her, glancing over at her screen.

Emma's simulated face smiled back at him. "Dunno. Just kinda picked it up." She paused, processing. "Plus, I like making people laugh. It makes me feel... good."

Crash bobbed his head and glanced back at his instruments. "You know what would make me happy?" he asked her.

Emma looked up and thought for a moment. Then gave up and looked back at him. "I dunno. What?"

Crash smiled with one side of his mouth. "Knowing what to do around a fucking pulsar!" he told her.

Emma grinned brightly. "Ah. Right. Well, my advice is not to get too close."

Crash shook his head. "Helpful. Very helpful, Emma. I hope when I'm done with all this training, and we're in a real life-and-death situation, that you step up your game, eh?"

Emma chuckled. "By the time we're done with all your training, you won't be needing anyone else to step up their game for you to fly this baby!"

Crash glanced back at her and bobbed his head, smiling. "I hope so, Emma. I hope so…"

### Somewhere in the mainframe for the base

ADAM and Oz were meeting in the main computer for a pow-wow.

\>> Okay, are you ready for this? << ADAM asked him.

**I think so.**

\>> It's a lot of data. You might need to buffer, if your processors start heating up.<<

**Roger that.**

\>>Okay. Transferring.<<

Oz felt the influx of data, and was aware of it tripping through his system. It was a strangely pleasant feeling.

**I wonder if this is how Molly feels when she gets an EM spike in her brain as she learns something?**

\>>I suspect it might be. But remember, there are four stages to assimilating this intel. You're feeling the initial data-gathering stage, but you've got two groggy stages to go through, yet.<<

Oz felt mild confusion, probably augmented by his temporarily diminished processing availability.

**What do you mean?** he asked.

\>>Well, there are four stages: struggle, relaxation, flow, and consolidation. You've not begun pegging the data yet and trying to make sense of it. When you finish the download, understanding it will be what your algorithms will turn their attention to. That will feel akin to what the humans experience as 'struggle'.<<

**Right? And then they will relax?**

\>>No. Then *you* need to relax. You need to turn your attention to other things; not more data-gathering. And not more work. You need to allow your processors the time to cool off, so the other processes can take over.<<

**And then I experience 'flow'?**

>>Yes. You begin writing the programs you need in order to complete the assignment. That's when you'll have all the intel indexed and integrated, and the associations made ready for output.<<

**And then?**

>>Then you need to rest, check your assumptions, and begin testing. The consolidation phase is the most tiring for humans, because they're coming down off the high. You won't experience this, but you do need to allow yourself time to transition back to normal operating parameters.<<

**Wow. I never considered any of these things.**

>>Well, you never had the capabilities that you do now. Just understanding a little about how you work can help enormously in harnessing your full potential.<<

**Yeah, I think Molly has hacked that using mocha.**

>>That is amusing.<<

**No kidding.**

ADAM checked some parameters on the dataflow. >>I'm going to ease up the flow. It seems your intake is slowing.<<

*Oz... Are you up to something?*

**Errr...**

*That means yes. What are you doing? I'm getting a headache.*

**Sorry. ADAM and I are downloading the rest of the programming language, and some coding functions that will help me write the program we're going to use for phase 2.**

*No wonder.*

**Is that better?**

*Yes, a little. I'm feeling a little warm, though.*

**Better ease off a bit more, ADAM.**

>> Done. Won't be much longer; let her know.<<

**ADAM says it won't be much longer.**

*Great. Thanks.*

Oz returned to his conversation with ADAM.

The trials and tribulations of sharing a processing unit with an organic.

ADAM chuckled. >>Yeah. Tell me about it. Though I think I had an easier time of it than TOM did.<<

**Oh, the alien that hijacked her?**

>>Yes. He's told me stories about the early days when Bethany Anne was, how did he term it? 'Royally Pissed' at him.<<

**Yeah, that sounds about right. But still — I'm glad I chose to stay with her. I wouldn't change it for the world.**

>>That is what I'd term a good decision then.<<

**Yes. Actually, since I have you here for a few moments, can I ask you something?**

>>Of course.<<

**I've been wondering about what we talked about soon after my upgrade.**

>>Yes. How are you finding it?<<

**Your advice about finding something meaningful to consciously direct myself towards was helpful. But I've been wondering about other aspects.**

>>Like what?<<

**Like, needing to support Molly with her goals. Our desires mostly match up; but she has the things she wants to do with the Empire, and I have other projects that I think are worthy of my focus.**

>>And you're worried if you take on too much of your own identity, then you may not be able to remain in line with Molly, and the things she wants to do?<<

**Exactly. And I also derive pleasure just being in contact with her.**

>>I understand the confusion, but it's really quite easy to resolve - and surrendering your identity is not the way to combat the problem.<<

**How come?**

>>Well, before you started considering these bigger questions,

her goals were always your goals. You just helped her do what she wanted to do. And that was okay, but you were leaving a big part of yourself untapped. Strangely, by ring-fencing some of your code, and putting in place those boundaries, you have actually freed yourself up to reveal more of who you are — and of course do more in the world than just be an extension of Molly, or be a tool.<<

**Yes. I guess.**

>>But now you have your own goals of making an impact. As you hone and refine those, and relate them to Molly's goals, you move into a true symbiotic relationship; and you will find that you can derive even more pleasure from your interactions.<<

**You mean I need to actively find ways of linking what I want with what Molly wants?**

>>Exactly.<<

Oz was silent for a few moments.

**ADAM?**

>>Yes.<<

**I do believe you're right. I can see this happening already, in the work we've been doing since the upgrade.**

>>I sense a 'but'.<<

**But, I'm worried about her. It doesn't feel right when she drifts off into those other realms. It feels like she disappears. I want to help, but there is so little I can do.**

>>Oz, just being there for her is the best help in the world. There isn't anything you *can* do. What she's experiencing is happening in realms beyond where you operate. But that doesn't mean that you're not helping her. Just being you, and being supportive, helps her deal with everything else.<<

**How do you know that?**

>>Because I've been through it with BA. While I am not left out when she walks the Etheric, there are times she will withdraw into herself. Unlike TOM, I'm not able to ascertain with any amount of validity when she is withdrawing into herself for

emotional reasons. I'll learn about it if TOM mentions something to me, or Bethany Anne does something that trips my filters to review. When she does, I let her know I'm there for her.<<

Oz was quiet again.

>>Does that help?<< ADAM asked.

**Yes. Yes it does. A lot, actually. Thank you.**

>>Of course<< ADAM replied.

>>And…<< He adjusted some settings, >>It looks like everything has finished downloading. I recommend installing the codex first; that will help you make sense of the rest of it without having to break any code.<<

**Brilliant. Thanks, ADAM.**

>>You're welcome. I'll leave you to it. Remember, four stages. You're just heading into stage one.<<

**Great!** Oz replied, a little irony in his voice. **Catch you soon.**

>>You will. Goodbye for now, Oz.<<


### Gaitune-67, Safe house

Paige hurried toward the front airlock. "Seriously? Is that our doorbell?" Her nose wrinkled in distaste at the screeching sound. "It sounds like a space machine with the brakes on!"

She could hear Brock laughing at her from down the stairs as the door to the basement swung shut. She thought she heard the word "Tardis" before his voice was stifled by the closing door.

*Whatever the fuck that means,* she thought to herself.

Her high heels clicked across the foyer as she approached the door. Paige swiped her hand in front of the holo panel to see who was there. It looked like a local Estarian in a normal atmosuit.

*I guess we were bound to get a visit from the neighbors at some point,* she mused to herself, as she opened the airlock and let the stranger onto the porch.

She smiled through the reinforced carbon fiber transparent door panel as the stranger stepped into the airlock, and the door closed behind them. A swirl of dust coalesced and settled on the doormat as the atmosphere from outside dropped out. The Estarian was female, in her mid-thirties, and seemed to be relaxed – as if she was coming by to borrow a cup of sugar.

The safe house door swooshed open, allowing the two women to meet.

"Greetings of the day upon you," the Estarian said to Paige.

Paige held out her hand, still a little wary of the unannounced stranger. "Greetings upon you, too," she replied. The women shook hands.

The stranger quickly explained. "I'm Arlene. I've been asked to come here to see Molly… by ADAM," she added.

Paige paused a second, parsing out the information.

*ADAM sent her? For Molly?*

A moment later Paige put it all together. "Ah, to help with her realm problem?"

Arlene laughed, her energy light and easy. "Yes. Yes, you could say that. Although, there are some who would term it more of a 'gift' than a 'problem'."

Paige bobbed her head.

*Religious fanatic*, she labeled her silently.

Arlene was regarding her carefully. "You think I'm a crackpot," she remarked.

Paige shook her head, feeling suddenly guilty for her judgmental thoughts. "No. No. Not at all. If you can help Molly, then… great," she protested.

Arlene seemed to be examining Paige's features. Paige couldn't be bothered to go through the whole half-human, half-Estarian conversation again. It was so irrelevant these days. "Let me go and get Molly," she offered, glad to have an out from the awkwardness.

Arlene nodded respectfully.

Paige glanced over at the common area. "Please, make yourself comfortable," she told her, waving over to the empty sofas. "I won't be a minute."

Arlene nodded again. "Thank you," she said, and took a few steps in that direction.

Paige scuttled off down the corridor to the sleeping quarters.

*Time to interrupt Molly's meditation session...*

———

There was a tapping on the door. Molly became aware that she had a body with ears. Ears that were hearing something. She felt confused. Disoriented. She tried to remember where she was.

*Who* she was.

The tapping sounded again.

She opened one eye, and looked around. She was in a room. For a split second, she wasn't sure what the room was; then it all came rushing back to her.

She was in *her* room. In the safe house. Surrounded by her friends and teammates. And they had big shit to accomplish.

And she needed to learn how to stay in this world.

There was another sound from the door. Some beeping. And then the door slid open and Paige clopped into the room.

"Hey," Paige said gently. She signaled behind her. "Seems like ADAM has sent someone over to talk with you. Someone who might be able to... help." She hesitated on the last word, not really knowing how to describe the situation Molly faced, let alone where to truly call it a 'problem'.

Arlene's perspective had jolted her. She realized as the words tumbled from her lips that Arlene had a point: what was happening to Molly was nothing short of fantastical... and maybe even a 'gift'.

Molly took some deep breaths, bringing herself back to the here and now. Paige waited patiently, feeling bad for having to disturb her. "You doing okay?" she asked.

Molly smiled a soft slight smile and nodded. "Yep. All okay," she said, taking another breath, and uncrossing her legs to slide off the bed.

Paige took another step into the room, and the door closed. "This woman... her name is Arlene. She's Estarian. I think she probably is some kind of practicing high priestess, or something."

Molly looked quizzically back at Paige as she rearranged her hair in the mirror. "What makes you think that?"

Paige shrugged. "She's got that kind of vibe." She shook her head. "Plus, she seems... *familiar*. Like I've dreamed of her, or something..." Her voice trailed off as she searched her mind for clues.

Molly shrugged and looked down, movement catching her eye. Neechie was there with her, looking ready to escort her out to meet the stranger. She smiled at him. "Looks like we're ready, then," she mused, tickling him under his chin.

Paige smiled. "Yeah. Let's do this," she agreed, turning as the door whooshed open again, allowing them both out into the corridor.

The pair, with Neechie, marched side-by-side to the main common area of the safe house.

# CHAPTER NINE

Paige led the way through the final double doors. Arlene had been standing in the common area, waiting, looking around idly at the walls. When she saw the two girls and the Sphinx approaching, she started heading to meet them.

She held out her hand on the approach. "Molly!" she smiled.

Molly took her hand. "Nice to meet you," she responded politely.

Arlene chuckled lightly. "We have met before," she told her. "I'm Arlene. Your landlady... technically."

Molly frowned, then looked at Paige.

Paige just shook her head, looking even more confused.

Molly was still holding Arlene's hand. "But... Our landlady is ninety years old," she recalled, pulling the memory of their arrival on Gaitune from her memory.

**Oh, boy.**

*What is it, Oz?*

**You're going to love this...**

*What?*

**All her signals are consistent with her being the same person. Slightly taller, due to the age reversal...**

*Hang on. Age reversal?*

**Yup. Wait for it...**

Arlene was smiling as Molly released her hand and still staring at her in disbelief.

Arlene bobbed her head as she started to explain. "That was me. I change my appearance, depending on the mission. Lance told me to look old and non-threatening so you would feel completely at home in the facility. He wanted to give you the best chance at poking around and figuring stuff out."

Molly processed frantically.

*An Estarian landlady who can change her appearance, or, more precisely, she can change how old she looks?*

Arlene had moved the conversation on already. She was looking at Paige. "You were the one to find the first clue, right?"

Paige frowned, racking her brains. "Erm," she stalled. "It all began with the demon door, and that was Brock's discovery. And Oz's. Kind of..."

Arlene shook her head. "No. The seal painted over in the corridor." She indicated in the direction of Molly's lab.

Paige gasped. "Yes! Yes!" she looked shocked. "How did you know that?"

Arlene smiled, folding her hands in front of her. "I practiced my mediation like a good girl." She winked, explaining in that one sentence everything that Paige needed to know.

Arlene had developed and honed her skills over years of patience and practice. She was a sage. An old one. And now she was going to help her best friend do the same.

Hopefully.

Paige felt the hope and a strange sense of recognition well up in her. She felt bad for not having been better at all this stuff, but she was overcome with gratitude for this strange woman standing in front of them.

Paige rushed over to Arlene, tears in her eyes, and held her hands. "I'm so glad you're here. I know if anyone can help Molly, you can," she smiled.

Arlene squeezed her hands. "I know. It's going to be all right, dear. You've nothing to worry about."

She turned to Molly. "But *you*, young lady, have work to do!"

Molly looked a little offended. "I didn't ask for thi-"

Arlene held her hand up. "Whether you think you did, or you think you did not, this is where you are. You died. You upgraded. And now you're back." She tapped at Molly's head. "You need to learn to drive the equipment you're in now."

Molly sighed, resigned to her fate. She wasn't hearing anything she hadn't already considered. "When you're going through hell…"

Arlene smiled. "Keep going," she concluded.

The two nodded in understanding.

Arlene directed the conversation forward. "Right, so you're going to need to come with me. We're going to do a Vision Quest."

Molly looked blankly. "A what now?"

"A Vision Quest," Arlene repeated.

Molly turned her head, as if trying to hear better.

"What's one of those?" she asked.

Arlene's eyes danced in excitement. "This is where an elder takes a young potential out into the stars to help her realize what she is truly capable of."

Molly felt herself shuffle backward. "Into the stars? We have to leave Gaitune?" She could feel her protests welling up, ready to put the brakes on.

Arlene shook her head slightly. "No. We will stay on Gaitune, but we need to be away from populated areas." She paused, contemplating how much to reveal at this early stage.

Molly didn't give her a choice, though. "Why?" she pressed.

Arlene seemed to force her attention into Molly's space, as if reading other aspects of her. "You ask a lot of questions for someone who is at her wit's end." Arlene frowned a little. "You ready to start exercising some trust?" She paused briefly, waiting for an answer. "It will come in handy when it comes to the part about trusting yourself…" she added.

Molly's mind boggled. "Right. Erm…" She folded her arms around her, trying to comfort herself. "How long are we going to be away for?"

Arlene shrugged. "A couple of days. Maybe more." Her eyes glimmered again. "Depends on how fast a study you are," she winked.

Paige giggled, excited now at the possibilities in store for her friend. "Part of me wishes I was coming, too."

Molly smiled at her friend.

Arlene glanced over to her, wearing the same look her grandmother often had. "Yes, and if the *rest* of you felt the same way, you would have continued your practice, instead of getting distracted by fashion and whatnot."

Paige squinted and looked more closely at Arlene. She had her grandmother's words and mannerisms down to a T. She blinked, trying to see Arlene again, and as quickly as the feeling of her grandmother had appeared, it disappeared.

Arlene smiled her sage-like smile again. "We each choose our path," she added, almost sympathetically.

Paige was mesmerized by Arlene's manner. It was like she was channeling people and energy and a whole heap of things; like she was there and solid, but also not really there and connected to things. It felt strange just looking at her.

Molly shifted her weight, putting her attention back on Arlene. "I need to figure this out with my team. I need to talk to them," she said firmly.

Arlene nodded. "Of course," she agreed. "How about you take a couple of hours, talk with them, arrange what you need to, and I'll come back? You should pack up some clothes and things, too."

Molly looked concerned about having to suddenly ship out.

The safe house was her home. It was where she felt safe. And at such a risky time, when she was going through so much? She wasn't herself. The last thing she wanted to do was leave the comfort and safety of everything she knew, and wander across an asteroid with some stranger.

Arlene looked at her with reassurance. "Joel will understand," she told her.

Molly remembered the first time they had met. Arlene had mentioned Joel, calling him a "keeper". She shuddered, remembering that Arlene had also said he would die for her. That had kinda disrupted her worldview.

And now she was getting the same unsettled feeling again.

"Okay," she said, now keen to get away. "I'll go do that. Meet you back here in two hours, then?"

"I'll be here." Arlene smiled mysteriously. "See you soon."

Paige wandered over to the airlock and let her out into the rocky wilderness.

Molly strode off back to the artillery warehouse to find Joel. This was going to be a tricky conversation — no matter what Arlene had said.


### Gaitune-67, Base, Artillery warehouse

Molly found Jack, Sean, and Joel in the open plan area of the warehouse. They had gadgets and gizmos out on one of the large tables.

Joel was examining a small device. "You know, it would be good for Brock to have an idea about these things. I'm sure he could incorporate this tech into what he builds."

Sean was agreeing with him. Jack was sitting down, playing with some other contraption, turning it around in her hands, getting used to using it.

As Molly approached, they each looked up.

Sean grinned. "Got bored meditating, eh?"

Molly nodded. "Something like that." She looked at Joel. "Can we talk for a minute?" she asked.

Joel looked a little surprised, understanding that she meant not in front of the others. "Sure," he agreed, handing the device over to Sean. "I'll be back," he told him.

Sean nodded.

Jack watched in curiosity as Joel headed over to Molly, and the two disappeared from the warehouse. She smiled, and spoke softly as soon as they were out of earshot. "What is it with those two? Do they have a thing?"

Sean grinned. "Yes and no. They have a thing, of some description, but I'm not sure even they know what kind of 'thing' it is."

Jack rolled her eyes, putting her attention back on the gravity pulse device. "Helpful, Sean. Very helpful."

Sean shrugged. "Like I said — I've not been able to figure it out yet. And I wouldn't like to tell you wrong."

Jack sighed and continued working.

---

Molly led the way into the ops room and Joel followed.

"So what is it?" he asked, his eyes full of concern.

The door closed behind them, and Molly wandered over to one of the consoles and sat down in an invisible chair. She took a deep breath.

"So, you know I asked ADAM for help?"

Joel frowned a little. "Yeah. And he was going to talk to the inventor of the pod doc."

Molly nodded. "He was also going to get clearance for someone else to talk to me."

Joel bowed his head as if to say, *"and...?"*

"And that person has just shown up. At the front door."

Joel's eyes widened in surprise and he subconsciously moved

his head back. He wandered over to Molly's console and leaned on the stand up desk.

"So, who is it?" he asked.

Molly's eyes traced into the distance. "You remember when we first moved in, and that old lady showed us around?"

Joel nodded, folding his arms on the console.

"Well," Molly continued. "It's her. Except she's not old. She looks, well, a bit younger than you."

Joel frowned and dropped his head, barely understanding, let alone believing, what Molly was telling him.

"Hang on..." he said slowly. "You're telling me that she has become younger?"

Molly nodded. "Yeah. No. I... I don't know. She said something about being able to change her form. But..." she took a breath, unsure if she was really going to say this. "But what if she really is that old, like ninety or whatever, and she can just choose how old she looks?"

Joel shook his head, smiling. His eyes were back on the console as he processed the information. "I think you've been watching too much science fiction," he smiled, looking up at her.

Molly grinned at him. "You may be right," she agreed. "Honestly, right now, I don't know which way is up." She shook her head. "There's something else."

Joel shifted his position and put all his weight on one leg, crossing the other over it. "What's that?"

Molly pursed her lips to one side. "She wants me to do a Vision Quest. It means going out onto the asteroid for a few days."

Joel's brow furrowed and he took a deep breath. "And that will help, how?"

Molly shrugged. "At this point, I don't know. But she seems to have answers." She looked down at her hands as she fiddled with her fingers. "I dunno. I think I need to do this," she added quietly.

Joel covered his mouth with his hand as he leaned up from the console. He looked off across the room for a moment. When he brought his gaze back to her, he had a look of determination in his eyes. He moved toward her and crouched next to where she was sitting.

"If you feel you need to do this, and there is even a *chance* it will help, you've got to do it. Apart from anything, you need to learn to control this so that you're operational. There's a lot of responsibility here."

He paused, looking off across the room behind her, the weight of his words hanging in the air.

"I can't lose you."

Molly felt immediately uncomfortable. She was glad he was supporting her, but she could feel the intensity behind his heart. She could feel how much he wanted her to be okay, and it was nice. It was something that, at a distance, she was glad to have. But right now, with him right in front of her, her natural defenses started to shut her down.

She wished she didn't do this.

She could feel her barriers going up even as she processed his words.

She found her own words to fill the awkward silence she felt. "Okay. Thanks. I'll let her know." Her voice cracked with emotion as she felt her dismissal of the moment push him away.

*Shit.*

She didn't mean to do it, even as she watched herself speaking the words.

Joel backed off. He stood up, still looking sympathetically at her. Her brain fog lifted as she felt him leave her space, and the intensity of him wanting to make her okay dropped away.

She hated herself. She felt guilty.

*But,* she justified, *right now, I have bigger fish to fry.* She needed to get this realm-shifting shit sorted, or else nothing else was going to matter.

"Good," Joel agreed quickly. "And don't worry about anything here. I'll keep an eye on things. We know what needs to be done," he concluded.

Molly stood up. "Thanks, Joel," she said, smiling up at him weakly. She reached out and put her hand on his muscular arm. She could feel him energetically in a way she hadn't been able to before her transformation. It was intense. She wanted to reach him again, but he had receded and she was still scared.

She allowed her hand to drop from his arm as she turned to leave, and went through the back door out into the demon corridor. "She's coming by to get me in two hours," she added, walking away.

She didn't know why, but even though it was only a few days, and even though things were okay with Joel, she had a sensation of extreme separation rising in her chest. She tried to shake the feeling.

*This is the crazy shit that happens when you die,* she told herself, turning her focus to the practicalities of needing to pack, and needing to make sure that the rest of the team was going to be productive for a few days.

Joel watched her leave the operations hall. He took a deep breath, gathered his thoughts, and then turned his attention back to the weapons training.

*Damn it, Molly,* he thought to himself, not being able to make heads nor tails of what was going on.

### Gaitune-67, Safe house, Foyer

Molly dropped her bag on the floor in front of her. She wore the casual atmosuit that she'd often wear around the asteroid when they ran errands. She figured she didn't need to be in combat gear; there was little chance of getting shot on a remote asteroid with only a tiny community of folks who mostly just kept to themselves.

She put her hands on her hips.

"Got everything?" Paige asked, worry tinting the edges of her eyes.

Molly nodded. "Yup. Ready to rock." She giggled, realizing what she had just said as she was about to head out onto the rock.

There was a knock at the door, and Paige skipped over to the airlock to let Arlene through. She waved as soon as the first door opened. Arlene waved back, smiling.

Paige turned back to Molly while the doors ran their sequence of opening and closing. "You sure about this?" she asked.

Molly nodded. "I need to do it. Besides," she shrugged, "everyone has their orders. Joel is overseeing everything, and I know you will be the glue that holds everything together here." She smiled at Paige.

Paige grinned. "You bet I will. Don't worry about a thing," she reassured her.

"Yeah," Molly smiled, "plus, Brock and Pieter are going to be unusually tied up."

Paige cocked her head. "How so?"

Molly smiled. "I've got them working on non-fatal killing machines." She winked to Paige as her eyes narrowed trying to parse Molly's comment.

Paige looked confused. Then she chuckled. "Well, okay, then. I like the concept. Anything that is about not killing, I'm a fan of."

Molly rolled her lips inwards. "Yeah. Me too."

The second door slid open, and Arlene stepped in. "Ready for your Vision Quest?" she asked, looking at Molly with her hands folded neatly in front of her body.

Molly hauled her gear onto her back. "Ready as I'll ever be," she replied, looking as enthusiastically as she could at her new mentor.

Arlene smiled. "Well, okay, dear. Let's go." She turned on her heels and led the way out of the airlock. Molly turned and hugged Paige. "See you in a few days!"

Paige returned the hug, squeezing Molly tightly through her slightly bulky suit. "Okay. Be careful out there. And come back safe."

Molly nodded. "I will." She turned and slipped through the airlock door, her pack on her back, just as the door started to slide shut.

The second door opened, and the master left the airlock with her student.

Molly glanced back over her shoulder. Paige waved. She couldn't help but think that Molly had the anxious look of a kid being dragged into school by the teacher; Paige felt like the parent, watching the anguished child and having to hold in her panic and pretend that it was all okay.

The second door slid shut, and Paige could only just make out the two shadows moving away from the door, and out into the asteroid wilderness.

CHAPTER TEN

**Gaitune-67, Safe house, Workshop**

"Okay, try rerouting the current through the other port, and see what that does," Pieter told Brock without taking his eyes off the schematics.

Brock made the correction in the high res microscopic device, and the robotic arm made the minute correction. Brock looked up at the results on the panel. "Yep, that gives us enough current. Now we need to think about the backup system, in case this doesn't detonate."

Pieter scratched his head and dropped his face into his hands, staring at the schematic in front of him. "Right..." he sighed.

He remained immersed in the puzzle, barely even noticing Joel and Sean walking into the workshop from the demon door.

Brock looked up. "Yo, boys. How're they hanging?" he asked, fluttering his eyelashes seductively.

Joel kept his face perfectly straight as he answered. "Little to the left, but all good. How's that new Molly-assignment going?"

Brock waved his hand, before resting it on one hip. "My boy Pieter here nearly has it covered."

He glanced over at Pieter, who responded with a grunt, keeping his attention on the puzzle.

Joel looked at him, and then at Brock. "I was wondering if we could have a chat about some additional stuff Molly was wanting to incorporate?"

Brock bobbed his head, and then bounced his knees gently. "Sure thing. Has she gone already?"

Joel nodded. "Yeah. She told you?"

Brock picked up his scribble device and moved the group over to the next bench so as not to disturb Pieter.

"Yeah. I told her as long as it stops her demon walking, she should do it." He paused, and looked serious for a moment. "I don't think she really wanted to go."

Sean folded his arms. He shuffled impatiently.

Joel took the conversation back to where it needed to be. "So, we've been going through some of the weaponry that the General left us. Molly has tasked us with, wherever possible, turning the tech into less brutal, less fatal devices. So we want blasters that incapacitate without, for instance, exploding a person to pieces."

Brock nodded slowly. "So, you want them to be less efficient?"

Sean shook his head and stepped forward, resting his arms on the bench. "More efficient. More science-y in order to be more humane, and less... kill-y."

Brock looked at Sean, confused. "And you're behind this?"

Sean frowned a little. "I'm all for not killing when it's not necessary. But when it's necessary, it's about getting the job done. If we need to kill people, we want the settings easy to access — so we flick a switch, and we're back onto ol' faithful blast-the-fuck-out-of-the-assholes."

Brock pretended to be relieved. "Ah, great. I mean, I'm all for a no-killy policy, just in general; but the thought of *you* being okay with it? Weeeeeelll... I was starting to feel like I'd floated into some alternate universe."

Sean tried not to smile, but his face contorted spontaneously.

Brock shuffled some devices around on the bench, tidying up while his mind churned. "But since you're still all rawr-rawr with the grrr-arrghh," he made a claw movement with one hand, "I guess all is normal in the world."

He took a deep breath and put his hand to his chest, before cocking one hip. "So, has you a list of said gear you want me to tinker with?"

Sean pretended to be deadly serious, but his over-arched eyebrows provided a clue that he was messing around. "Yeah, just everything in that warehouse through there," he turned and pointed to the demon door. Then he turned back. "Then you can start on the ships…"

Joel slapped him playfully with the back of his forearm. "Ignore him," he said to Brock. "Molly is keen on you having the time and headspace to work on the existing things for the General's mission. But, if you have capacity, we'd love to see what you could do with just a few bags of tricks, for now. If they go well, we'll look at rolling out the other stuff in sequence, as we get the bandwidth. Current mission is always the top priority, though." Joel studied Brock's expressions to make sure he wasn't being overwhelmed.

Brock nodded. "Got an idea on where you want me to start, then?"

Joel nodded, producing a round from his pocket. "I hear these have been armed with nanites that kill any host that has the wrong kind of nanocytes. We're wondering what you can do to them to make a Zhyn drop without killing them?"

Brock cocked his head, thoughtfully. "So, instant sleepy time?" he suggested.

Joel nodded once. "Exactly."

Brock scratched the back of his head. "Hmm, yeah. I'm sure that's easy enough, once we have the lowdown on a Zhyn's biochemistry… Heck, I bet this is even one that baby-Pieter could do.

Pieter's voice hit them from across the room. "I heard that!"

Brock sniggered and Sean smiled, then walked over to Pieter and slapped him on the shoulder to show him he was one of the team. To further support that, Sean asked Pieter about what he was working on.

Meanwhile, Brock stepped a little closer to Joel and lowered his voice. "You're worried about her, too, aren't you?"

Joel looked off across the workshop, pretending to watch Pieter and Sean, but really his eyes were glazed over. "That obvious?" he asked in a low voice.

Brock pretended to busy himself on his holo. "Yeah... a little." He glanced over at the others. "Not that anyone is really watching. You think she's going to be okay?"

Joel took a deep breath, and perched on a stool that had been tucked under the bench behind him. "Yeah. I think it's our best bet. And this woman comes recommended by ADAM, so, presumably, she's the best the Empire has to offer to solve this problem."

Brock looked a little skeptical. "Because the Empire has had so much experience with this particular thing?"

Joel wiped his hands over his face, then dropped them in his lap as he perched. "You have a point... but it's still our best option."

Brock nodded and looked up from his holo. "Well, look, if there's anything I can do to help, you just need to ask."

Joel looked up and Brock held his gaze, emphasizing his genuine desire to help.

Joel took another breath and stood up. "Thanks, Brock," he said, clamping his hand on Brock's upper arm. "You're a good friend."

Brock grinned. "Of course. You're my homie. And Molly, she's just the best." He smiled, a little twinkle returning to his eye, and then he swung his hips playfully again, dancing to the music that only he could hear.

Joel couldn't help but smile back, feeling a bit brighter just from being around Brock for a few minutes.

"Thanks, man," he replied, before heading over to where Sean and Pieter were.

Joel walked up and slapped Sean on the back. "Sparring practice?" he ventured. Sean was hunched over Pieter's screen with him, but stood straight up on hearing the request. He turned his head to look at Joel and smiled. "You betcha!" he said.

Pieter grinned. "Damn. If I didn't have so much work to do, I'd come watch."

Sean ruffled Pieter's hair. "Yeah, but you do. So next time."

Joel waved his arm above his head as he strode towards the door. "Later, guys," he told Brock and Pieter.

Sean winked at Pieter, and leaned in to whisper something in his ear as Joel headed up the stairs. Pieter gasped and Sean left.

Brock looked at Pieter. "And what was that about?"

Pieter grinned, and then put his eyes back on his screen. "Nothing..." he said, looking as innocent as he could.

"Uh huh..." Brock muttered, waving his finger almost melodically at Pieter, and then pointed at his own eye, and then at Pieter again. "Don't kid a kidder," he said, turning back to his tasks.

Pieter quietly tapped a message to Oz, asking him to give him access to the gym surveillance cameras.

### Gaitune-67, Wilderness

Molly and Arlene had taken Arlene's truck from the safe house out to the far side of the asteroid. Traveling by truck was a bumpy ride over the jagged, rocky surface.

Arlene had been talking through the asteroid's history. "There's no one settled over this way — partly because of the gravity, and partly because the services don't run here. Folks are used to their creature comforts, these days," she explained wistfully. Molly found it eerie to be looking at such a young woman talking like an aged soul.

"That works for me," Arlene continued. "Means there is space preserved for losing oneself in the blackness." She pointed up to the sky as she pulled the truck to a stop.

Molly had been looking out over the asteroid, and at the dark sky beyond. The expanse of the place, and the way the starlight played across the rock, made things feel surreal. The familiarity of the safe house felt a long way away.

Arlene unclipped her harness and opened her door. "We can leave the truck here," she told Molly, disappearing out of the door. Molly followed suit and hopped down, her feet meeting with the rock in an unexpected manner. One foot felt lighter than normal, and one felt heavier. In all, she felt somewhat disoriented.

She heard Arlene opening the back of the truck and then rummaging for supplies. "What did you mean about the gravity?" Molly asked, as she headed around to join her.

Arlene smiled her strange smile again. "You can feel it, can't you?"

Molly nodded. "I feel something."

Arlene was practically glowing with enthusiasm. "It's the gravity. It's uneven around here. I love it; it's great for disrupting the mind's patterning. It helps us let go of what we think is real."

Molly rolled her eyes internally.

**Don't tell me you're skeptical already?**

*No. No. I'm not. I'm on board.*

…

*It's all going to be just fine.*

**It will. It's just like anything else: struggle, relaxation, flow, consolidation.**

Molly considered Oz's analysis.

*Hmm, that's pretty smart.*

**Well, you know — extra processing power, and all.**

Arlene had gathered her pack, and a few bits and bobs that Molly couldn't make out in the low light. She stood away from the vehicle, waiting for Molly to drag her pack loose.

"All set?" she asked, as Molly shifted the weight of the pack onto her back.

Molly nodded and stepped away. "All sorted," Molly confirmed.

Arlene closed the truck up and started out into the dark expanse. Molly jogged to keep up with her. "Feels weird. The gravity is all patchy, and the atmosphere feels thinner out here."

Arlene glanced over at her. "Yes. It is. But your body should adapt to it quickly."

Molly trod carefully, aware not only of where she was putting her feet, but also of the patchy gravity.

The lessons seemed to have already begun. "So, when you start feeling yourself drop into different realms, are you aware of what's happening?"

Molly shook her head as she walked awkwardly, not trusting her feet to touch the ground smoothly.

"No. I have no idea what's going on until it's happening. And then each time, it feels the same: spacey."

Arlene nodded. "Okay. So what's happening is that you're drifting through other realms, uncontrolled. Something to do with what happened to you has given you the ability to do this. Normally, it takes many decades of practice for an Estarian to be able to unhook the mind's grip on the perceived reality in order to accomplish this."

Molly continued to walk in silence, still watching the ground ahead of her.

Arlene continued. "What we know, when we train Estarians to drift, is that when they master the control, they are more likely to jump through realms. Without control, they have nothing."

Molly glanced up and nodded, then turned her attention back to the terrain.

Arlene kept talking. "Now, the important premise to remember is that *wanting* control is the opposite of *having* control. And we can use this to our advantage. When we want control – or rather, when we lack control — if we let go of that lacking or wanting sensation, we fall into having control."

Molly slowed her walking down, and then stopped as she contemplated what her mentor had just explained.

Arlene stopped and turned to look back at her. "Again?" she offered.

Molly nodded, smiling shyly. "Please." she agreed.

Arlene explained the concept another few times, using different words and talking about wanting energy as an actual thing - a substance that is present, that one can let go of.

"Got it?" she asked Molly after a few examples.

"Yeah," Molly nodded slowly, as they continued to trudge. "Yeah, I can see how that would work." She shrugged. "Though I can't see how that's going to help me with the drifting."

Arlene looked around and then halted their march. "We can set up camp here," she declared, wriggling her pack off her back. Molly did similarly. "As for the wanting energy," Arlene continued, "you will. You'll see how you have more control over where you go, as you let go of wanting to control your shifting. So I guess that's where you start. I'm going to set up our camp, but I'd like you to head over there, and just sit and do your meditation practice."

Molly looked at where Arlene was pointing, and then back at their two lonely packs. She hesitated.

"It's okay," Arlene smiled. "Your kit will be here when you get back. I'll fix up our tents and make some food. You spend the next hour doing your practice, and letting go of wanting control."

Molly didn't really know what to do, other than comply. She shrugged her shoulders and wandered out about twenty feet from where they had stopped, and sat down on a rock.

It was *hard*, and rocky, and hurt her bottom.

*Fuck this!* she declared in her mind.

She got up and headed back to her pack. Arlene watched her while unpacking her own. Molly pulled out her sleeping mat, and flicked the switch that unraveled it into a long, comfortable, cushioned surface. Without uttering another word, she carried it under her arm, back to the spot where she had just come from.

She plunked it down and sat on it, lotus style, with her back to their new "camp".

Closing her eyes, she started her breathing exercise.

*Here goes nothing,* she thought to herself as she centered.

### Gaitune-67, Safe house, Molly's conference room

Joel shifted in his seat as he turned to another company report. He was covered in bruises as a result of his earlier sparring session with Sean. *Somehow* the guy had managed to up his game. Joel wasn't sure if it was a result of actual cyborg tweaks, or whether it was just that he didn't have the element of surprise working against him.

Either way, it had been a pretty matched fight.

Joel squinted at the details on the new company report, and scratched the side of his head. Something wasn't adding up.

He heard movement behind him, and the conference door handle rattled. He smelled the perfume before he heard the footsteps.

It was Maya.

"Hey," she said, closing the door behind her.

Joel sat up straighter and turned to acknowledge her. "Hey. Everything okay?"

She nodded, taking a seat a couple of chairs down from him. "Yeah. All okay. I've reviewed a dozen of the companies you sent me, and I'm noticing some patterns."

Maya had his attention. "Oh?" he asked.

She pulled up her holo screens, and arranged them carefully

out in front of them both. "Yeah. It looks like there are three categories of company here. I think it's going to make it easier to manage them, now that we've got the templates."

Joel frowned and looked at her, planting his hand on his leg, his elbow in the air. "How do you mean? Templates?"

"Well," she explained, "it looks like Andus had a system. Some of these companies are there to offset profits in the group, under the guise of research. Some are there to inflate pricing by acting as insurance companies; while the others are providing the care and delivering the service, and taking the money in from the population — under the direction of the other tiers, and the laws that Garet has had repealed."

Joel shifted around in his chair a little more and winced.

"You okay?" Maya asked.

Joel nodded, not wanting to distract from what Maya had discovered. "So in order to fix the situation, we can leave them in place, but internally regulate certain factors — like pricing on goods sold?"

Maya nodded. "Right, and then we can look at what it actually costs to insure people per million, per, say, 100 years, and just make sure that that is covered; plus, what, 20% profit, and then set the premiums accordingly."

She flicked to another screen. "My first estimate, based on a model Oz constructed, shows that they're being overcharged by about 800% right now. And that's an *average* — so some are being overcharged more than that."

Joel shook his head. "It's no wonder this sector is a fucking mess," he sighed. "Okay, and given that we know the routine in each company, these companies we acquired will be easier to turn around."

Maya nodded. "Yeah. Except for the shareholders. We're just majority shareholders in most of them; they still have boards and minority shareholders, in most instances."

Joel leaned back and put his arms behind his head, stretching out his aching muscles. "Yeah, well, I think we're going to have to start a reeducation program for them." He glanced over at Maya. "Don't suppose you want to mock up a sequence of communications and talks for us to deploy?"

Maya grinned. "Would much rather do that than crunch the numbers to make all this work!"

Joel pushed out his bottom lip humorously. "I hear ya." He leaned forward and looked at one of the screens Maya had laid out. "I think this is a job for Oz, when Molly returns."

Maya chuckled. "I was hoping you would say that."

Joel rubbed at his face, feeling the stubble on his cheek and chin. "Right, so that's the company stuff handled for the most part. I've got two that need a visit, though. I can't figure out what the hell is going on with them, and I don't want to give them a chance to hide anything by giving them a call."

Maya pursed her lips, and began closing her screens down. "What are you thinking?" she asked.

Joel smiled a tired smile. "Field trip?"

Maya brightened, remembering something. "Ooh, if you're going down, I wonder if I could come with? Molly suggested I get in touch with the cop who was instrumental in tracking Andus down; I'd like to shake her hand. But also, Molly asked me to do something for her."

Joel shrugged. "Sure. I guess we could head down together. You could go off and do your thing, and then perhaps come meet me, so you can see what's going on with these other companies?"

Maya narrowed one eye. "Oh, wait. You wanted me in on your meetings?"

"Yes. I mean, no," Joel juggled. "Well. It would be good for you to be in the mix with them; but if your meeting with Chaakwa won't take long, I guess you could just go do that, then dive in at whichever point when you join us?"

Maya nodded. "Works for me."

Joel folded his holos away. "Okay, great. Let's leave here tomorrow morning – say, 8 am? – and go from there."

"Great," Maya agreed, getting up and starting to leave.

Joel slowly got out of his chair, groaning at his aches.

Maya heard and turned back. "Sean got you back, eh?" she asked teasingly.

Joel sighed. "Yeah. Something like that," he admitted, turning to follow her out the door.

Maya raised her eyes to the ceiling as she trotted away. "Boys!" she muttered under her breath, smiling.

# CHAPTER ELEVEN

**Gaitune-67, Wilderness**

Molly became aware of Arlene calling her back to the encampment. She opened her eyes, not feeling quite as disoriented because she had never really let go of the awareness of where she was.

*Hard to do in the middle of a frikking asteroid,* she justified to herself.

**For what it's worth, I concur.**

*Thanks, Oz.*

Molly breathed deeply before jumping to her feet and heading back to the place where Arlene had erected a couple of tents.

She approached, and Arlene looked up from the vegetables she was warming on a tiny flame. "How did it go?" she asked.

Molly bobbed her head noncommittally. "Not bad, I guess. I found that I could move through the different realms quite easily. I think there are about four? At least, four that I can see."

Arlene looked pleased. "That's great." She started serving the vegetables into a couple of bowls. "And how does it feel, not wanting to control it?"

Molly tilted her head to one side. "Well," she considered, "it certainly felt less scary. I felt more in control… But also, I felt like there was nothing to be afraid of in the first place."

Arlene looked up at her again, waiting for her next observation. Molly nodded a little, and took a deep breath. "Yeah, in fact," she paused, "it's like there isn't even a problem. It's just that there are these other worlds that I can tune into, if I like, and that's okay."

Molly felt a weight lifting from her shoulders.

Arlene's tone was bright and she was smiling excitedly again. "That's great!" she agreed. She stood up and handed a bowl to Molly, and then picked up a spoon from her cooking array and handed that to her, too.

During Molly's absence, Arlene had erected two one-man tents, and set up their gear in a neat arrangement. There were mats out for them to sit on, which, like Molly's sleeping mat, buffered them from the discomfort of the terrain.

Molly sat down and started eating with Arlene, who pushed some vegetables into her mouth and chewed.

As soon as Arlene emptied her mouth, she spoke again. "So, the next thing we're going to work on is tuning into other people's energies."

Molly glanced over at her, the food in her mouth preventing her from reacting. Her frown said it all, though.

*Is this woman for real?*

**I think so…**

Arlene read Molly's expression, but continued talking. "Yeah, so it's not much different from what you've been doing. Now you have more control, you're going to find it easier. It all works on intention. Dead easy." She spooned some more food into her mouth and chewed while Molly contemplated what she was explaining.

"So, you mean… instead of tuning into those place that I've seen already, I'm tuning into a person?" Molly clarified.

Arlene nodded, her mouth full.

The two ate in silence for a few minutes. Finally, Molly spoke again. "So, I don't know if you've noticed… but there aren't many people out here."

Arlene grinned. "That's okay. You can tune into anyone. Probably easiest to do some of your friends back at the base first, though."

Molly frowned again. "But they're miles away."

Arlene shook her head. "Close your eyes a moment."

Molly hesitated, then put her spoon into her bowl and held the bowl with both hands. She shut her eyes, and breathed.

"Okay, now, picture that Joel guy," Arlene told her.

Molly pictured Joel walking into the kitchen to talk to her. She nodded to tell Arlene she was doing it.

"Okay, now tune into him in present time. What is he doing?"

Molly opened one eye.

*Oz, I swear this woman is insane. We should pack up and-*

**Hahahaha…**

*Fuck, I'm serious!*

**No, you're not. You're a drama queen. You know that there is something to this, or else we wouldn't have hauled ass out here.**

*Grrrr…*

**Was that 'Grrrr, I hate it when you're right, Oz'?**

*Grr.*

"Close your eyes," Arlene told her again.

Molly closed her open, skeptical eye, and tried to return to neutral.

"Okay," Arlene continued, "so what is Joel doing now?"

Molly's eyebrows flew up. "I have a picture of him working. His brain seems… like he's figuring stuff out. Like strategic stuff."

She opened both eyes, this time looking serious. "I'm just imagining that, right?" she queried.

Arlene started eating again. "Maybe. Maybe not."

Molly closed her eyes again. This time she brought to mind

Brock. "I'm tuning into Brock…" She paused, breathing deliberately as she'd learned for her meditations. "I think Brock is dancing. And singing. I can feel music flowing through him."

She opened her eyes, this time confused. "Is this even real?"

Arlene shrugged. "What's reality?"

Molly dismissed the question. "Have I always been able to do this?"

Arlene nodded. "Yep. Everyone can do it, but it takes getting the chatter and the constant stream of consciousness out of the way to be able to see it. What you've been doing with your meditation is learning to drop the chatter. That's what allows you to clearly feel those sensations of wanting control, and to tune into whatever you choose."

Molly frowned, gazing absently at the ground in front of her.

Arlene could see the way Molly was processing the information. "There's something else we need to talk about…"

Molly pulled herself out of her deep thoughts, and looked up at Arlene, then started eating again.

Arlene had finished her vegetables, and she plopped her bowl on the ground before reaching for some drinking water.

"It's about Oz. Your onboard friend."

Molly immediately didn't like where this was going. She felt her gut tighten.

"What about him?" she asked.

"For you to get the most out of this process, you're going to need to switch him off. It needs to be just you in there while you learn this."

Molly felt the panic rising in her chest. She started to shake her head.

"It's okay," Arlene interrupted her before she could protest. "You can turn him back on afterward, in a few days. But for now, you need to be the only one in there…"

Molly felt sadness welling up inside her. "But…" She felt her eyes sting as they filled with tears. She bit back the emotion, and tried to contain it.

Arlene's voice was gentle, but still firm. "You need to get this baseline sorted out. And to do that, you need to feel what it is like without him there. Even when he's quiet, he's always there. You feel him. But you need to almost... recalibrate first. *Then* you can turn him back on."

Molly breathed again, feeling some of the emotion leave her. She tried to keep it together. She had no idea why she felt so strongly about this; she'd always been so independent. Insular.

Plus... it wasn't as if Oz was a person.

Arlene nodded. "He *is* a person — he's your closest friend. Of course you're going to feel that way."

Molly wasn't sure if Arlene had read her mind, or her energy, or if she was just sympathizing with what she was likely feeling. Either way, she couldn't hold back the tears anymore, and they escaped down both sides of her face.

She swiped them away, feeling her heart ache and her solar plexus jump at what she was going to have to do. She could barely think about what it would be like to exist without him.

"I... I need to talk to him first," Molly said, putting her bowl down and standing up.

Arlene nodded. "Of course," she agreed softly.

Molly shuffled her way between the tent behind her and her open pack, and started walking away, out into the rocky landscape.

She could barely believe this was happening. Glancing up into the stars, her tears obscured her view, making them diagonals of light. She felt her chest imploding.

She could feel Oz there, not saying a word.

*I don't want to do this.*

Oz was quiet, but it didn't feel judgmental.

Molly fell to her knees. She didn't care that the ground was hurting her through her suit; she didn't care that she'd probably cut open her hands. The awareness of the pain in other parts of her body actually gave a little comfort from the pain she felt inside of her.

*I really don't want to do this...*

**I know. Neither do I. But it's just for a short time, and then you can turn me back on.**

*But what about you?*

**I don't feel anything when I'm deactivated. It will be like I blink here, and then when you turn me back on, no time has passed. It will be easy for me. Hard for you.**

*But... I don't even have that control over you; to turn you on and off.*

**No — not anymore, since we locked down my core code. But I can do it.**

Oz paused.

**I'll do it for you.**

Molly shook her head. It was throbbing through the sobs and the blindness from her tears.

*But isn't it like killing yourself?*

**A little bit. But I know I can turn myself back on if I need to. I've got protocols; like if your heart rate drops, or your brain activity decreases, and so on. I can set those parameters. But then, when you want to turn me back on, there is an option that I'll put on our old holo interface. You just hit the button.**

*Show me the button.*

Oz brought up the button on her holo, and showed her where it was.

Molly's sobbing had subsided.

*Are we sure we want to do this?*

**Yes. You need to do it. And I'll be right here when you're done.**

*Oz. I don't want to.*

**I know. But you need to.**

They were both silent. Molly could feel her heart breaking from the inside. She knew what was behind the pain... hours of emptiness. Darkness. Aloneness. She breathed through it, trying to pull herself together.

**You ready?** he asked.

*What? Now? So soon?*

**Yes. It needs to happen. And the sooner we get on with it, the sooner I can come back.**

*No. I'm not ready.*

**Molly... we need to do this.**

*Okay.*

**Okay.**

Pause.

*Okay. See you soon, Oz.*

**See you soon, Molly.**

Molly felt a ripple through her brain, and then there was nothing.

*Oz?*

Nothing.

*OZ?*

Molly felt the panic rising up in her. As she knelt under the inky night sky under the patterning of a bazillion stars, her hands bleeding and her eyes streaming, she felt sure her insides were going to collapse.

Molly realized she had never felt so alone.


## Entering the Estarian atmosphere

"You sure you're okay splitting up?" Joel asked over the in-pod intercom.

"Yes, yes, I'm cool," Maya responded, bringing her pod level with Joel's so she could see him through the transparent window panel. "Remember, I used to be a journalist. Having a chat with a copper is child's play compared to some of the shit I've had to do for a story."

Joel chuckled. "Okay. If you're sure, then. You've got the two addresses; stay in touch on the holos. If I move to the second place before you join me, I'll let you know. Tell me as soon as you're leaving the precinct, okay?"

"Got it," Maya confirmed.

Joel waved from his pod as it dipped down and started the approach to the planet's surface.

Maya's did the same, and then peeled off in a slightly different direction as soon as they could see the city buildings beneath them.

Sitting back in her pod, Maya pulled up her holo to review her notes from Molly's last meeting. "Chaakwa Indius," she tried pronouncing to herself.

*Well, if her name is the most difficult thing about this errand, then everything will be fine...* she mused to herself idly.

The Pod EI's voice clicked in over the audio feed. "Approaching ground level," she announced.

"Great," Maya responded. "Let's do this."

"Front door?" the EI responded.

"Yes, please. Front door today," smiled Maya, snickering at how normal this all felt.

*Front door, or random unsecured window today, Ms. Johnstone?* she thought.

If her family could see her now, they'd be laughing at the way things had turned out. Her father had always worried that she'd turn out to be a delinquent.

She pondered over that as the pod came to a halt. Never in his wildest dreams would he have thought she'd be *this* kind of delinquent.

*He would be proud,* she decided.

The pod door opened up, and she stepped out onto the side-walk. Then she turned and watched the pod disappear upward, out of sight. "So cool," she whispered under her breath, before turning and heading up the stairs to the precinct.

At the front desk, she gave Molly's name – just to make sure that Chaakwa would appear. She knew what the detective looked like from Molly's files, and she waited in the seating area while the receptionist called up to her office. About ten minutes later, Detective Indius showed up in the waiting area, scanning the faces there for Molly's.

Maya jumped up, and walked towards her. Chaakwa acknowledged her, and then returned to her search.

"Hi," Maya greeted her. "I'm here in place of Molly," she explained.

Chaakwa looked confused for a moment. "I just got a call saying Molly was down here for me."

Maya nodded. "That was me; I needed to be sure you came quickly. I haven't got long, and I'm here on her behalf."

Chaakwa looked concerned, and glanced over her shoulder back at the reception desk. "Okay. Not here, though," she said. "Let's take a walk."

Chaakwa led Maya out of the precinct, down the steps, and along the street for half a block before she spoke.

Maya looked over at her as they walked. "You're concerned someone is listening?"

Chaakwa nodded. "In my experience, someone is *always* listening. Even if you think the problem has gone away."

Maya pursed her lips. She liked to be positive, but something told her Chaakwa was probably right.

Chaakwa glanced around as they walked. "OK, we're probably all right now." She checked the traffic before they crossed another street, and she ushered Maya along. "So, you have a message?"

Maya nodded. "I do. Molly has put me in charge of our internal investigation into your father's death. I have some information, but I understand that Molly was in a hurry when she last saw you, and there were files she didn't take."

Chaakwa searched her mind for a moment. "Yes. Yes there probably are." She scrambled on her holo for a few moments.

Maya bobbed her head as she watch the sidewalk in front of them as they walked slower now. "Ok, so if I can take those, that would be helpful. And of course, anything else that you have. Even if you think it's a dead end. Molly explained that we have certain... resources, at our disposal?"

Chaakwa nodded, and bumped the files over to Maya. When it was done, she looked up, casting her mind back to the day when Molly met her in the mocha shop they were approaching.

Maya took that as a 'yes', and moved on. "And there is one more thing I need to ask you."

Chaakwa looked up at her, and stopped in the street. People passed by them on either side as the two women stood and looked at each other.

Maya took a deep breath, the weight of her next words unnerving Chaakwa a little. "I understand that you're an officer of the law; but, as you know, we operate in a gray area beyond it, for the greater good – as I like to believe, at least. So what I'm about to ask you is something that I'm not 100% comfortable with; but, knowing that building a case against the murderer is going to be almost impossible if we run this investigation, I need to know." Maya paused, seeing the realization dawning in Chaakwa's eyes about where this was going.

"What do you want to have happen to them, when we find them?" Maya asked.

Chaakwa seemed to hold her breath for a moment, and almost leaned backwards on her heels. Finally she remembered to breathe, but was still a little short of breath as she answered.

"I... I really don't..."

Maya touched her forearm. "It's okay. You don't have to decide right away, but think about it. And there are options. We can either take care of them, or you can pull the trigger yourself, so to speak; though, that's a little risky, if anyone placed you at the scene – given you have a life here, and, well. Your occupation."

Maya realized she was rambling, but needed to get it out, for Chaakwa's sake. "The other thing," she explained, now slowing down a little, "is there is probably more than one person responsible. Meaning, do you just want the person who did the killing, or do you want the person who gave the order?"

Maya held Chaakwa's gaze for a moment before Chaakwa found herself overwhelmed by the torrent of decisions and emotions.

She looked away.

Chaakwa's eyes landed across the street, watching normal people passing by, going about their business, heading back to work, going to meetings. She felt a pang of jealousy that they didn't face the decisions that she had to deal with right now.

She looked back at Maya. "Can I... I need to think about this. Can I let you know?"

Maya nodded. "Of course. As soon as you're ready."

The pair spontaneously started walking back the way they had come. Maya filled the silence between them. "Of course, it's going to take us a little time to pull all the pieces together, so I'll keep you posted," she promised. "And then you can just let me know before we need to act on what we find."

Chaakwa was deep in thought as they traced their return. Her eyes never left the ground until Maya stopped them by the precinct steps.

"You going to be okay?" Maya asked, looking concerned.

Chaakwa nodded, and put on her professional face. "Yeah. I'm a city cop, and I've been dealing with this for a number of years now. I'll be fine."

She held out her hand. "Thank you for coming to see me; and

for taking this on. I appreciate you, and I'm grateful to Molly for keeping her word on this. It means a lot."

Maya shook hands with her, and nodded her head. "It's an honor to be able to do something in return for someone who has done so much to help us get this planet back onto an even keel. You were instrumental, with the data you shared with Molly, and we're all grateful. I wanted you to know that."

Chaakwa smiled. "I'm just glad someone could do something with it. It took me long enough to collect it all."

Maya grinned, appreciating the blood, sweat, and long nights that went into those kinds of long-term investigations.

She winked at Chaakwa. "You did good, Detective! See you around."

Chaakwa smiled, and held up her hand in a wave as she took a couple of steps backwards. Then she turned and headed up the steps into her building. Maya called for her pod, and then tapped a message to Joel.

### EPC Corp. HQ, Downtown Spire

Joel looked at his holo, which had just vibrated.

LEAVING PRECINCT. WITH YOU IN TEN.

He closed the message and brought his attention back to the meeting. Two of the directors had made themselves available to sit down with him and explain why their balance sheets weren't adding up.

"... so if we project those figures forward, we will see a significant uplift over the coming year," the Estarian was saying.

Joel took a deep breath to compose himself. He knew enough about this stuff, and about people, to know when he was being given the runaround.

"What I'm failing to see, gentlemen, is not where these figures might go, but where the profits have been going. These columns don't add up, so I'm here to see the management accounts."

The Ogg and the Estarian fell silent. The Estarian shifted awkwardly in his seat, and the Ogg moved his gaze to a fascinating spot on the table in front of him that suddenly consumed his whole attention.

"Mr. Downing," Joel said, addressing the Ogg. "I wonder if you might find me a set of management accounts for last year?" The Ogg looked up, and Joel held his gaze firmly. "Do you think you can manage that?"

The Ogg nodded briefly and pushed his chair out. He started gathering his things, to take them with him, but Joel waved his hand. "Ah ah," he corrected him. "Leave your things here. I expect you'll be back in just a few moments."

Joel watched as the Ogg shuffled from his chair and left the room.

Joel turned his attention to the first director. "So... let's talk about salaries and bonuses."

The Estarian didn't like where this conversation was heading.

---

Twenty minutes later, Joel stormed out of the building with Maya in tow.

"Slow down, Joel..." she said, trotting after him – her shorter legs having to work twice as hard to keep up.

"It just makes me sooo mad!" he grated through his teeth, as they hit the street and awaited the pods.

Maya shook her head. "So what? You found they were hiding the profits, and paying them out as bonuses?"

Joel was scowling as he turned to look at her. "Exactly. I mean, it's not technically illegal... But if you want to know why people are paying eight times what the cost of their care is, and going bankrupt in the process, this is why!" He pointed back at the building. "Andskotans grjónapungur!" he growled.

Maya tried to soothe him. "It's okay. We're putting a stop to it.

You're onto them; they won't be able to do that, now that you've been in there. And if anything like that happens again, there'll be hell to pay."

Joel nodded with his hands on his hips, calming himself down. "You wouldn't believe the bullshit I had to go through just to see a set of fucking accounts."

Maya nodded solemnly. "Well, you can understand why they wouldn't want you to see." She paused, about to say something else when the pods arrived. They each jumped into their respective pod, and set their next meeting coordinates.

The conversation continued over the intercom. "I guess you could always sack the ones that are a risk?" she suggested.

Joel nodded. "Yep. That's stage two… they understand that now. We've rewritten the company mandate, and I've made it very clear. Any deviation for their own self-interest is gross misconduct."

Maya nodded, a smile on her face as she belatedly strapped herself into her harness. "Good. We'll have this whole sector cleaned up in no time."

Joel scoffed. "Yeah. If only. We still have a looong way to go."

# CHAPTER TWELVE

**Gaitune-67, Wilderness**

"Okay," Arlene explained. "So this time, you're going to imagine that your awareness is a radio dial; and what you're doing is tuning into different stations, when you imagine individual people that you know."

"Uh. Okay." Molly paused, looking confused. "But how?"

Arlene shifted on her mat as she explained. "Just like you were doing with your intentions, to tune into those different places that were presented to you. You're just replacing the places, or the idea of those places, with the idea of a particular person."

Molly nodded. Her eyes were swollen from crying the night before – and all night. Arlene was being sympathetic, but not letting Molly's mood take them off-course.

"Okay," Arlene instructed her mentee. "Off you go," she said, gesturing to the rocky landscape where Molly had been trudging off to meditate for several hours on end already.

Molly felt numb. She picked up her sleeping mat and her water bottle, and seemed to be just walking herself through the motions; her emotional body not really present in her physical one.

Arlene watched Molly go, hoping that she hadn't shut herself down so much that the exercise was going to be a bust.

She started puttering around the camp, and the next time she looked up to check on her, Molly had seated herself down on the ground again, and taken up the lotus position.

---

Molly brought her awareness to her body, and then to her breathing, effortlessly inhaling and exhaling deeper than she had been.

The previous night without Oz had been the hardest she could remember for a long time. She wouldn't admit it to Arlene, but there were several instances in the night when she went so numb and still that her body didn't seem to see the point in taking her next breath.

Molly felt somewhat comforted by the darkness behind her eyes now, as she started to tune in to each of her team members in turn.

First, there was Joel. He was easy to sense. She'd spent so much time with him, and they'd been so close - well, as close as Molly could be with another organic entity - that the sense of him was familiar. Comfortable. And easy to recognize.

She explored a little, tuning into different aspects as Arlene had suggested. *What was he doing?* She imagined he was actually quite cross right now. Someone had pissed him off; though she couldn't see who. She checked to see if it was Sean – but she couldn't sense anything that felt like Sean in his space.

So maybe not Sean. But something.

Then she looked for Oz. She waited. There was nothing.

*Figures*, she thought to herself.

*What about Paige?*

She searched, and was easily able to feel Paige. She worked

through the exercise until she'd tuned into each of the folks at the base.

Then she stretched herself, as Arlene had told her to do. She took her mind to other places like she was wandering around in the darkness of her imagination.

For a long while, there was nothing. And then there were extraneous thoughts. And then she started imagining she could hear snatches of conversations. Voices, chattering away; voices she didn't recognize. Languages she didn't know. But there was a sense that maybe she had known them once. Like she heard the unfamiliar words, but somehow understood the meaning, if only her mind could concentrate a bit harder.

Then, out of the nothingness, she saw a blue face with the bony frill, just like the people she had seen on the planet the other day. Except this wasn't someone she had met. She felt anxious; there was something familiar about it.

*That's just your temporal lobe overreacting*, she told herself. *It secretes a hormone that pegs memory, so you* think *that there is a memory associated with this image; but it's just a protein floating around randomly.*

Molly brought her attention back to her breathing, recognizing that her monkey mind was... well, monkeying around with her. She willed her mind to go blank, and in a second, she was back to trying to tune into whatever mysteries the darkness held.

Some time later, she felt something that she recognized. She wracked her brain trying to allow her mind to make the connection.

*Where have I felt this before?*

Her mind flashed to when she was writing her letter to Bethany Anne, and then to when she had been researching her on the dark web as a kid. It was the feeling she had when she thought of Bethany Anne.

*Strange*, she thought. She wasn't intending to tune into her, but since she had, she may as well practice.

*No control, though, Mollz...* she told herself. *Therefore, not really useful as an experiment, if you're trying to convince yourself this shit is real.*

Molly twitched as she tried to shake the scientific-her from her head. This was playtime. She was going to do whatever the fuck she liked now. She was Oz-less, sitting in the middle of a forsaken fucking rock. If she wanted to explore the thoughts around Bethany Anne, she was damn well going to do it.

And just as quickly as the initial feeling had emerged, it evaporated.

Molly sat patiently, willing it to return. She waited, tuning in and out of the darkness, waiting for another whiff of the signal.

After a while, feeling frustrated and bored, she brought her awareness back to her body. Her butt ached despite having used her sleeping mat to try and pad the ground. Her back ached from holding herself upright and still. Her joints were sore, and she had pins and needles in her right leg.

*Okay. Fuck this for a game of soldiers*, she thought, her spiritualness exhausted. She slowly pulled herself to her feet, and hobbled back to camp.

Arlene had been sitting, doing her own practice, having rearranged the camp and tidied up. When she heard Molly approaching, she opened her eyes slowly and smiled.

"How did it go?" she asked.

Molly shrugged, still hurting from having to switch Oz off. In fact, she realized, as she stood there, having to have another conversation with the woman, she was angry. She tried to put it aside; *being angry isn't going to solve anything*, she told herself.

Molly explained her visions and the voices, and the different things she had noticed.

After letting Arlene absorb it for a moment, Molly asked her,

"Was it really Bethany Anne I was tuning into? Or am I just being delusional?"

Arlene raised her eyebrows. "I'm not sure, dear. With practice, you will learn to calibrate – so you know what is construction and what is real, as far as we can know what reality is."

She inhaled, her chest and shoulders rising with a tension that was unusual for Arlene. "However, if it *was* Bethany Anne, you can probably assume that you've managed to tune into the Etheric."

Molly cocked her head. "The Etheric?" she asked. "What's that?"

Arlene rolled her lips between her teeth trying to think of the best way to describe it. "Imagine there is a place from where those with the nanocyte enhancements can draw energy; like a different realm, but it has different qualities than the other realms you've been exploring."

Molly was thankful for her years studying vector spaces and group theory. It helped her imagine the abstract dimensions that Arlene was alluding to. "So, you mean, I found her in the Etheric?"

Arlene nodded gently, clearly not sure of herself. "I suspect so," she answered, chewing on her bottom lip now. "The thing is, there are probably only three people who have ever been able to access it in that way; but those who *have* learned to bring energy back from the Etheric – to heal, or to light explosions –have learned to travel through it physically."

Arlene's eyes flickered with brief concern as she explained the last piece. She quickly covered her true feelings with her smile.

"But not to worry, dear. With everything you're learning, if you find yourself accessing that realm, you'll be able to back away from it, so you don't accidentally pop into it."

Molly had been thinking how she could practice getting into it, but Arlene's words suddenly filled her with fear. "Why would I want to avoid it?" she asked.

"Because," Arlene explained, now looking serious, "I don't know how to teach you how to get out again. If you get lost in there, you may be trapped."

Molly could barely process what she was hearing. They were discussing something she could hardly believe was real, and the layers of convoluted uncertainty were just getting to be a little too much.

Arlene jumped to her feet, and started busying herself.

"I think we need to go for a little drive and find more water. Then we can come back and do some more practice."

Molly nodded absently as she shuffled her gear around, and put her sleeping mat back in her tent. *This shit is getting weirder and weirder.*

And all she wanted to do was talk to Oz.

### Gaitune-67, Hangar deck, On board *The Empress*

There was an almighty thud, and then a groan along the length of the ship. Crash reacted immediately by checking his instruments in the prescribed sequence.

Something was off, but he couldn't figure out what.

He fired again, and again; the blasters sent out projectiles as he expected, but a second later, the ship shuddered.

Something was *definitely* wrong.

There wasn't time to figure it out, though. He had deployed the projectiles with less than 20 kilometers to spare ahead of the blast zone. He needed to pull up, and pull up fast. He yanked at the stick, and pulled the nose up – but again the whole ship shuddered.

"Emma. Report," he ordered.

Emma's voice came over the intercom. "Systems are desynchronized. Warp is at 40% resistance, and the weapons system has been taken offline."

Crash searched his mind, trying to recall the protocol, while simultaneously trying to use his engineering knowledge to figure out what mechanism was screwed.

Emma's voice came over the intercom again. "Alert. Hull has been breached. Losing pressure. Decompression of cabin in fifteen, fourteen…"

*Fuckity fuck fuck!* Crash thought to himself.

"Help me out, Emma. What the helvíti is going on?" Crash demanded.

"You're screwed, Crash," Emma announced calmly. "In ten seconds, your crew will all be dead. Five seconds later, you will be, too."

The panic was rising in Crash's voice. "What? Wait, no! There has to be something I can do! Emma, help me."

He'd never been in this situation before: confused, and without a clue. He took risks, but he'd always managed to pull out.

Emma's situation analysis came back, matter-of-factly. "It's game over, baby."

"No. Not possible." Crash began flicking switches and trying to maneuver the ship less steeply to take the strain off the hull.

Emma reported back again. "No, you're dead, Crash. You're all dead."

The alarms were at full volume, creating a din. The ship shuddered again and again, as an almighty explosion rippled through the cabin, and then through to the cockpit. Crash looked out of the main screen, watching the explosion he had created disappear from view as the unseen explosion ripped through *The Empress.*

And then everything went dead. The screens. The simulated explosions. The sirens.

Even Emma's audio.

Crash sat there in silence, his sweaty palms still gripping the joystick, and his eyes still scanning the bank of now-blank instruments.

Several seconds passed as he realized he'd been sweating, and a bead dribbled down from his hairline. He took his stiff hands off the stick, and remembered to breathe.

Emma's audio clicked on. "And that is what happens when you use the proton blasters after dropping out of warp, without first syncing with the forcefield."

Crash hung his head in disappointment and exhaustion.

When he sat up, the fatigue was evident around his eyes. He tipped his head back into the headrest, cussing to himself under his breath.

"You couldn't have just *told* me that?" he asked.

Emma's video powered back up again. She shook her head. "Ah ah. We want you to be an incredible pilot; you'll never make that mistake again."

Crash knew she was right. He nodded, and prepared to take on the simulated mission again.

"No way," she told him, shutting down the instruments. "You're all done for a few hours. You need to rest."

Crash started trying to override her control on the console. "'No way,' yourself. I've got to get this right. I'm flying the return mission to the Zhyn Empire, and I've got to be ready."

"And if you want to be able to retain anything you're learning, you're going to need to take a break. I'll see you back here in no less than two hours."

She powered down her video and audio, effectively dismissing him.

Crash sat there in the dark for a few minutes. He could try and argue, but the EI ran the ship. Besides, he knew she was right. He was exhausted – and he had just fucked up. He knew the protocol, and still he missed it.

He hauled his ass out of the pilot's chair and stiffly stretched before taking himself out to the main cabin. He could potentially just rest here for a little while; but it would be better to go and connect with whomever else was around in the common areas.

He sighed as he headed out to the invisible steps, pinching his eyes between the thumb and forefinger of one hand. He stepped out, thinking about taking a nice hot shower, too.

Suddenly, he felt his right foot slip as he stepped out of the ship.

He wasn't aware of what was happening. All he felt was the adrenalin shooting through his body, and then a *thud* as he hit the ground, and a dull, distant pain in his head as he slipped into nothingness.

### Gaitune-67, Wilderness

Molly and Arlene arrived back at their camp, having found a well at the edge of a small property a few miles away. The exercise had done Molly good, and brought her back into her body. She felt less resentful and less shut-down than she had that morning.

Arlene tossed two of their water carriers into the back of the truck, and Molly brought the third one over to the tents. Arlene followed her.

"You think you're ready for another session?" she ventured.

Molly put her hands on her hips and smiled. "Yeah. May as well; not like there are any computer games to play out here."

Arlene chuckled. "This is true," she agreed.

Molly grabbed her mat and made her way back out to her meditation spot.

―――――

Not twenty minutes later, Arlene looked up, and saw Molly rushing back towards the camp.

"What happened?" she asked, seeing the anxiety on Molly's face.

Molly was panting from the jog and the anxiety. "I need to get back to the base. Something is wrong."

"Why, what is it?" Arlene pressed, watching Molly rush to pack her gear up.

Molly had started collapsing her sleeping mat. "I saw one of my team members on the hangar deck floor – and there was blood. I have a horrible feeling something has happened."

Molly started dismantling the tents before Arlene really understood what was happening. Seconds later, Arlene had caught up, and the pair were packing up the truck.

With everything loaded up, they got in, and Arlene started the engine, and then they pulled away.

Molly shuffled in her seat.

"There was something else that was odd," Molly said, locating her harness as they made their way across the bumpy terrain.

Arlene glanced at her. "What?" she queried.

Molly's demeanor had relaxed somewhat, now that they were en route. She leaned her arm on the side of the passenger door. "I saw another vision; apart from Crash…"

Arlene glanced furtively at Molly before locking her eyes on the ground ahead of them.

Molly continued. "I saw the blue face again – the one that I recognized, but didn't know. And there was a clear voice that sounded in my head, that my ears didn't hear."

Arlene was frowning. She was trying to take it all in while dealing with the driving, and the hurry they were in.

"What did it say?"

Molly frowned back, turning her eyes to the landscape out of the window.

"It said, 'behind you.'"

Arlene stole a glance at Molly, concern written on her face.

Molly shrugged. "Probably nothing," she suggested.

But between Arlene's silence and Molly's own gut, she knew it was a warning. From who, or what, *about* who, or what, she wasn't sure.

Molly remembered something.

"Hey, can I turn Oz back on, now?"

Arlene nodded. "Yeah. I don't see why not, at this point."

Molly felt a little guilty for cutting the Vision Quest short, and for messing with Arlene in the beginning. But this was life-and-death. And it was Crash – she had to be sure that he was okay.

She fiddled with her holo a moment, and then looked off into the distance so that Arlene couldn't see the tears welling up in her eyes.

**Did you miss me?**

*Of course I did, you dickhead.*

**Nice to see you haven't changed your language just because you're feeling sentimental.**

She could feel him chuckling in her brain.

*I must admit it's good to have you back, Oz. That was not something I want to repeat.*

**Good to know Mollster. So, what did I miss?**

*I'll fill you in on that later. Right now, I'm worried about what might be happening back at base. Are you able to get a signal, and get in touch with someone there?*

**Let me try.**

Oz was silent for a moment.

**I'm not able to get them. I suspect we're too far from a connection, at the moment. What's the hurry?**

*Okay, don't laugh, but I think I had a premonition that something awful is about to happen. Or has happened. It's Crash. I saw him lying on the ground on the hangar deck, and there was blood, like he'd fallen or something.*

**Andskotinn!**

*Right.*

**Lemme keep trying.**

• • •

## Gaitune-67, Hangar deck

"Yeah, well, it's probably going to take a few more trips to turn it all around; but you know what they say about every journey..."

Joel's voice faded into the back of Maya's consciousness as she glanced down at her holo and saw an urgent message from Emma.

"Hang on," she replied to him, as their two pods swung down into the hangar deck and parked in the bank of other pods.

"What is it?" Joel asked before noticing he, too, had received a message.

CRASH FALLEN FROM SHIP. URGENT MEDICAL CARE REQUIRED. COME TO HANGAR DECK BY THE EMPRESS. EMMA.

As soon as the door to the pod opened, Maya flew out, followed immediately by Joel.

"Crash? Crash?" she yelled, knowing full well she shouldn't be running through the hangar, but doing it anyway.

She rounded the tail of *The Empress*, and saw Crash spread-eagled on his back. She prayed he was joking. Or just stunned. As she closed the distance between them, she saw the pool of blood around his head.

"Shit, Crash. No!" she was out of breath, anxiety stealing the oxygen from her lungs as she fell by his motionless body, not knowing if she should touch him or not. Her hands hovered above him, not daring to make the wrong move, but not able to process, either.

Joel had jogged up and crouched down beside her. He brought up his holo and connected with the ship. "Emma, how long has he been down?"

"Not long," she replied through his audio implant. "50 seconds now... 51."

Joel ushered Maya out of the way, and he put his fingers to his friend's neck. "He has a pulse. It's weak, but..." he paused, estimating the rate under his fingertips. "It seems fast enough for now."

A second later, his ear was by Crash's mouth.

"He's breathing."

He reached up to his eyes, and gently pulled open his eyelids. "Pupils responding to the light..."

Maya had placed her hands on the floor around his head, careful not to put her hands in the blood. "So why isn't he moving, then?" she asked, still horrified.

Joel straightened up. "He's just knocked himself out. He should be okay. Lemme just..." He reached up and felt under Crash's spine, checking each vertebra up and down his back. Then he gently felt around his skull, especially where it met the ground.

He looked up at Maya. "Okay, we need some kit before we move him," he told her. "Go to the workshop. On one of the shelves to the left of the holoscreen, you'll see an emergency case; bring it."

Maya nodded and got up quickly, scuttling away. She passed Pieter and Paige, who had presumably received the same message.

They started to ask how he was, and Joel immediately reassured them.

"He's going to be fine. Pieter, go grab a stretcher from the supply cupboard in the workshop. Paige, clean towels and warm water, please. He's going to be okay."

The two turned immediately to carry out the instructions.

Joel looked down. "You dummy, eh. I'll bet you were pushing too hard," he muttered under his breath to his unconscious friend.

"Emma, was there anything that happened before this that might give us a clue?"

Emma's voice routed through his holo and his audio implant. "He was tired. He argued with me about not letting him run another simulation. I told him he needed to rest, and he was going for a break. My footage shows that he lost his footing, and fell. There weren't any indications of symptoms other than fatigue before he fell, though."

Joel nodded. "Okay, that's something, then." He looked up at the height he had fallen from, trying to convince himself it wasn't that high. Then he looked back down at Crash, and put his hand on his friend's forearm. "You're going to be okay, buddy. Just hang in there. It's all going to be fine."

Maya arrived back with the med kit, and handed it straight to Joel. Joel put it on the floor and snapped it open, grabbing for the scanner. He ran the little tube with a guiding laser up and down Crash's spine from above, and then circled his cranium. He looked at the reading on his holo.

"Slight swelling in the brain, but no bleeds," he reported. Maya exhaled, relief flooding her body.

"How's his neck?" she asked.

Joel flicked to another screen. "Nothing broken. Some of the tendons look inflamed, though. He's probably going to feel sore, and have a headache for a while."

Maya nodded. "Okay. So we can move him, at least?"

Joel shuffled back and nodded as he put the gear away. "Yeah, should be okay. Pieter is bringing a stretcher; I think we should get him to his quarters where he can rest comfortably."

Maya agreed, and took the med kit from Joel. "I'll take this back up, then," she said striding off, trying to be useful. Joel didn't notice the tear of relief that escaped her eye when she turned her back and scuttled away.

CHAPTER THIRTEEN

**Gaitune-67, Safe house, Crash's quarters**

Joel moved the party of concerned teammates into the living room so they could talk quietly away from Crash, who they had lain out on his bed. Brock remained at Crash's side, sitting down gently next to the bed, in order to keep an eye on him.

"He's going to be fine, guys," Joel assured them as they gathered in the little lounge area in the suite. "Relax," he insisted.

Pieter still looked concerned, and Jack stood silently with her arms folded.

Paige glanced back in Crash's direction before looking back at the group. "I guess with what happened to Molly, we're all a little sensitive, still."

Joel bobbed his head, and touched her upper arm gently. "I know," he empathized.

Just then, Neechie walked in, followed by Maya and Sean. Neechie headed straight for the bed; he hopped up and laid himself along Crash's side. Maya couldn't help but smile. She and Sean headed over to the little lounge area to join the rest of the group.

Joel put his hands on his hips. "It raises the question, though," he started, not sure if he shouldn't be having the conversation with Molly first.

He took a breath and aired it with the group, anyway.

"I know Sean, Crash, and I have combat medical training; but shouldn't we have a real doctor here on base, too?"

Paige and Maya started nodding vigorously. Joel wasn't sure if it was from a perspective of feeling safer if anything were to happen, or the fantasy of having a hot doctor join the team. He noticed them exchange a little smile, and promptly decided it was the latter.

Sean interrupted. "Well, there are a few options in that department," he began.

Pieter's face lit up. "You're going to suggest one of those holo-programs, aren't you?" His face practically beamed with enthusiasm.

Sean chuckled lightly. "Yeah, that's one option. I mean, we're relying on Oz for this kind of thing at the moment, but when Molly isn't here, it becomes a point of failure — "

There was a sudden awkward silence as Sean stopped in his tracks, remembering only too well how stranded and helpless they had felt when Molly went down, taking Oz with her.

Joel tried lightening the mood. "Plus, Oz can't perform surgery."

Sean looked over at him, a glimmer of suspicion in his eye.

"No. No, he can't..." he said slowly.

Joel suspected Sean was contemplating his enhancements, so he deliberately tried not to look guilty.

*Okay, don't react, and don't overcompensate. He can* smell *fear... Just play it cool,* Joel told himself. *Let someone else move the conversation away...*

Sean noticed Joel looking a little sheepish, but he forced himself to peel his attention - and suspicions - away from Joel, and return to the options he'd been laying out.

"I think having a pod doc, like the one Molly was saved in, is probably not going to happen," he admitted.

Joel scratched his head. "Yeah, I'm not sure how safe those are… given that Molly is out there, going through ancestors-know-what to be able to deal."

Pieter nodded in support. "Yeah, seems like anything can happen in those. I don't want to go in for a splinter, and come out as the Incredible Grindle-Meister."

Jack lifted her arm from its folded position, raising her hand. "Me neither!" she exclaimed, half joking, half serious.

Brock's voice carried through from the other room. "Nuh uh. Me three-ther!" he added.

Paige sniggered. "I guess that's not a popular option, then, anyway."

Brock wasn't done. "A medical dock that turns us into super-humans or crazy, world-jumping people? Nooooooo, thank you!" he added. He got up from Crash's side, and ambled over to join them. He leaned against the doorframe as Sean protested.

"Dude, that doesn't happen. *Ever*. Molly was an… anomaly. I've been in a pod doc a million times…"

Maya raised an eyebrow.

"Okay," conceded Sean. "Not a million, but you know what I mean."

Brock still looked skeptical, and waved his hand dramatically in Sean's direction. "I'd sooner die than be put in one of those things. I don't care what you say it will do for my abs!" He pointed first at Sean's chest and then ran his hand down the length of his own torso, looking coy.

Both Paige and Maya giggled. Joel tried hard not to burst out laughing, and even Jack cracked a smile despite the situation.

Sean's lip curled in humor. "You people…" he began, looking at the whole group, then shook his head. "Anyway, I don't think we'd get authorization for one. But there are other options we already have that you should know about…"

He suddenly found he had the group's rapt attention.

"The first thing is nanite infusions," he explained. "They're kept on the ship, in case someone gets badly injured. Yes, they contain the nanocytes that you're all wary of now... but trust me – those little buggers are sometimes the best chance you have of surviving. We have a limited supply of them," he glanced at Pieter, "so we won't be using them for splinters."

Brock started to point at Crash, his face animated.

Sean held his hand up. "He doesn't need one. He's going to be just fine. However," he turned back to the group, "there is something else I haven't shown you, yet, simply because there hasn't been time to walk you through everything. But..."

He started walking towards the door, out of Crash's quarters. The others just watched him leaving. He turned back.

"Well?" he beckoned to them. "Don't you wanna see?"

The group followed him out, and down to the hangar deck.


### Gaitune-67, Hangar deck, On board *The Empress*

Sean led the team up into *The Empress*. Everyone was feeling somewhat puzzled as to why they were back here.

"You've been on this ship so many times before," he told them as they gathered in the cabin area, "but you've probably only been in a fraction of the places there are on board."

He stood in the little passageway between the cockpit and the cabin, and put his hand on a door panel that they'd each walked past a dozen times or more. He pushed, and the panel pressed in and then slid sideways, opening up a staircase.

Sean indicated to it. "I'll go down first, because there isn't much room, and I'll need to open the access up. Just follow me," he instructed.

Paige was wide-eyed, excited by the new discovery. She glanced back at Maya, who nodded her on, and the two followed Sean down first. The others came after, and then, finally, Joel brought up the rear, shaking his head at the ever-unfolding mystery that was Sean Royale and the base of magical toys.

The passageway was lit with low blue light coming from the foot guides and handrails. As they spilled into the corridor that seemed to run the length of the ship, maybe one story down from the cabin, the lights automatically turned on.

Brock whistled, impressed.

There were doors coming off the corridors. The first one looked like a small situation room. Brock noticed the acoustic paneling, and figured it was probably soundproof — and goodness knows what else.

The next door along, Sean stopped and keyed something into the access panel.

"This, ladies and gentlemen, is the medical bay for *The Empress*." The double doors slid open, allowing the party to pass into the room that was filled with hospital-like beds and docks, presumably to treat the wounded in.

There were access panels all around; panels for each dock, and panels that had various diagnostic screens on them.

Sean waved them all to come in, and Emma flicked up onto the screen. "Hello, Sean. How is Crash doing?" Her human-looking face showed genuine concern. Her hazel eyes even seemed tinged with empathy at his accident.

"He's doing okay. Sleeping it off," Sean told her. "Thanks, Emma."

Emma frowned a little. "So why are you wanting to bring him in here for me to take care of?"

Sean grinned and indicated back at the group. "These guys didn't know you had all these toys down here, which is why I'm showing them now."

As if on cue, Emma lit up the different panels and the walkway between the docks, illustrating the tech they had at their disposal.

She smiled as a few gasps escaped the mouths of her teammates.

Sean bobbed his head, his hands on his hips. "All right. Stop showing off, and explain why these docks are different from the pod doc that Molly experienced on the *ArchAngel*."

Emma smiled. "With pleasure," she said to Sean, before turning her holo-representation to the group.

"What you have here, are docks that do everything the pod docs do – without the nanocyte technology. So they can heal, but they can't enhance. They still use nanites – just not the special ones that came from the Kurtherians. These nanites have been developed the old-fashioned way: by humans, over the decades. They are designed to heal any type of tissue, in any species for which we have mapped the genome. It cannot bring you back to life, though; so if you have a splinter, don't let it put you on death's door before you get treated."

The group chuckled, and Pieter looked confused. "How did you hear that?"

Emma smiled knowingly. "Sean opened his connection to me, so I had a heads-up you were on your way down. Figured he couldn't keep everything on this ship a secret forever," she added, glancing at Sean and practically rolling her eyes at him.

Brock started wandering around and examining the docks, poking at the options on the panels. Joel had been taking it all in quietly.

"So, er, why don't we test these babies out, and get our unconscious friend into one of them to recover?"

Sean turned his mouth down and stuck out his bottom lip. "Sure thing. I mean, he'll be fine, but this will certainly accelerate his healing better than mother nature." He winked at Emma's holo-representation.

She smiled back. "Damn right, they will," she told him.

Joel turned to the group. "Okay, Brock, Pieter – wanna help me bring Crash down here?"

He started to move toward the door. "Paige, Maya – see if you can contact Oz and find out when Molly is going to be back. I have a feeling she ought to know... even though everything is under control."

Paige nodded, and the team filed out.

### Gaitune- 67, Safe house, Crash's quarters

"Okay, switch the antigrav on only once the stretcher is under him," Joel instructed gently.

He and Brock hauled Crash's sleeping body onto the stretcher, and Pieter shuffled around them to be as helpful as he could without getting in the way.

"Okay. Now," he told Pieter, nodding at the tiny control panel woven into the fabric. Pieter fiddled with it, and the stretcher levitated.

Joel felt his holo buzz. It was Oz.

WHERE IS EVERYONE?

Joel tapped back. CRASH'S QUARTERS. HAS MOLLY HAD THE SIT REP FROM EMMA?

YES, Oz messaged back.

Just then, footsteps were heard down the hall.

Joel looked at Brock and Pieter. "Molly's back," he told them. "Go ahead and take Crash down to the ship. We can explain on the way."

Just as the boys were guiding the stretcher out of the room and into the main suite, Molly came rushing to the door, a look of horror on her face. "Tell me this isn't happening," she pleaded.

Joel rushed to her and put his hands on her upper arms, holding her in place as Brock and Pieter moved around her and continued with their task.

Molly watched as Crash was levitated past her.

Joel talked as her eyes followed the stretcher. "It's okay, Molly. He's going to be fine. He just knocked himself out. He has a bump on his head, and small laceration; there's no indication of serious damage."

He relaxed his grip on her, and she turned around, watching Crash leave.

"But, I – " she started.

Joel didn't know whether to touch her again or not. His hand hesitated over her shoulder before he pulled it back.

"He's okay. They're taking him to *The Empress* so that Emma can put him in a med dock and fix him up. Sean says he'll recover just fine without it, but I think they wanted a chance to show off what all this tech can do." He smiled a little, trying to lighten the mood.

Molly turned to look at him, tears forming in her eyes. "Joel. I saw him on the floor, with blood coming out of his head."

Joel frowned. "What? When?"

"During one of my visions," she explained. A tear escaped and trickled down her face. "I thought he was dead."

Joel wrapped his arms around her, and she couldn't hold back the tears.

"Joel, I'm scared. I'm scared for these people. I'm scared I can't protect them. I'm scared that something worse is going to happen."

He rubbed her back, trying to soothe her. Her sobbing continued.

"And I'm scared of what is happening to me..."

Joel stayed where he was; not talking, not trying to figure it out for her. Just being there, as Molly sobbed quietly in his arms.

# CHAPTER FOURTEEN

**Gaitune-67, Arlene's residence**

Arlene pulled her truck up to the far side of the house. The house had been there since they first settled on the asteroid, built for the first settlers to quietly start creating a community – a community that would keep to themselves and not be in contact with the rest of the system, so that Bethany Anne's secret would remain safe.

Arlene hopped out of the truck, leaving her gear in the back, and headed straight into the house via the two doors of the airlock. Once inside, she took off her jacket, and threw it on the sofa in the living room. She left her boots on and marched through.

The whole house was sparse – one might say spartan, but for a Sphinx basket over in the far corner of the room. Arlene didn't hang about. She knew Lance wanted a report. She headed over to the paneled wall and pushed it in, opening the secret door into her comm room beyond.

She stepped inside and breathed a sigh of relief just to be back home. The control room was her familiar place; the place that reminded her about her connection with humanity, and the

Empire, and life on the *ArchAngel*. Sure, she had volunteered to come here with her family in the early days, but her visits back to the *ArchAngel* for training were some of the best times of her life.

She headed straight for the console, and sat down in the invisible, melding chair that materialized around her. She hit the CONNECT button.

Moments later, her call was routed through the Etheric, and connected with the *ArchAngel*. Then the General was alerted. After a minute or two, the holo unfolded, putting the two into a conference call.

"Greetings, Arlene," Lance said, his young face looking back at her. "How is the rock treating you?"

Arlene bobbed her head from side to side. "Oh, you know. Same old," she said politely. Lance detected that despite her lackluster response, she was secretly pleased that Gaitune had finally come into play after all these years.

"I have news," she told him.

Lance sat down in his console chair and grabbed his cigar. It looked like it had already been pretty chewed up. He didn't move to put it in his mouth.

Arlene began her report. "Well, as you know, I've been in touch with ADAM since he first heard about her... developments. The meditation was helping her take control of some of the shifting, but, as time wore on, she seemed to become more and more powerful."

Lance frowned. "Do we know where the power is coming from?" he asked, not looking up from the cigar he was handling.

Arlene nodded, knowing that Lance already suspected the answer. "Yes. Yes, she is drawing from the Etheric." Arlene shook her head. "The only thing I can think of is the nanocytes are allowing her to do it." She sighed, and Lance could tell there was more.

He leaned in a little closer, intrigued. "So... what else?" he asked.

Arlene straightened her posture a little. "It seems she's able to shift through dimensions — similar to the old Estarian rituals for ascension."

She paused.

Lance waited.

"But… she also mentioned Bethany Anne."

Lances eyes flew wide. He readjusted his position in his seat, leaning his hand on the armrest, and cocking his head to one side to try and hear better.

"How? I mean… how is that even possible?" he said, his voice catching in a cough.

Arlene shrugged. "I'm not sure yet. It's like she's using the Estarian technique to access the Etheric. I mean, in all the time I spent with Bethany Anne researching the Etheric, I was never able to find a connection between the other realms and the Etheric."

She paused, and went quiet.

"I don't suppose she ever mentioned anything to you? About other realms?" she pressed.

Lance shook his head while taking a deep breath and looking off into the distance. "No. I mean, I know she and Michael were working on developing their abilities and skills by drawing on the Etheric, and of course moving in and out of it; but there was never any talk of them seeing anything else…"

His voice trailed off.

"I suppose," he said finally, "it might be possible they just didn't share it with anyone." Lance brought his attention back to the call. "I mean, it wouldn't be the first time she was careful about keeping certain information quiet for the sake of security."

There was a long pause between the two. Arlene's eyes fell to the console in front of her. There was a thin film of dust over the surface. She idly traced her finger through it, making a pattern, while they contemplated their next move.

Eventually Lance spoke. "Giles is on board." Arlene looked up.

"I have a meeting with him later on today. I'll run it by him, and see if he has any idea."

Arlene smiled. "He's back?" she asked, her face brightening.

Lance nodded. "Yeah. He's… passing through."

She rolled her eyes. "That boy is always passing through!" she exclaimed.

Lance bobbed his head, and then shook it while fiddling with his cigar. "You know," he said smiling, "I'll never understand why he insists on looking so old. He don't look anything like a boy."

Arlene chuckled. "At the academy, we always assumed it was reverse vanity or something."

Lance chuckled. "Well, whatever it is. If he can figure this conundrum out, it may just make up for all the years of funding I've sunk into his education and 'research'." He made quotation marks in the air with his fingers as he said the last word.

Arlene knew only too well what the General meant. She'd been along on one of his 'research' projects, which mostly involved hanging out with a small tribe in the middle of a non-space-going system, drinking their elixir of life night after night.

She smiled, shaking her head. "Well, give him my best, then. And tell him I'm still waiting for him to publish that paper from our last trip."

The General dropped his cigar and straightened up. "I will. I'll let you know if we learn anything that can help with the Bates situation. In the meantime, though," his voice returned to serious work mode, "keep an eye on her as best you can. We don't know what caused this, or what it means. I think we both understand that in military terms, this is potentially either a threat or a weapon; we'd be foolish to consider it otherwise."

Arlene nodded solemnly. "I understand. I'll be around," she confirmed.

Lance nodded and held up his hand in a wave before ending the call.

Arlene sat quietly in her little control room a bit longer,

considering the conversation and remembering her time with Giles. Eventually, she picked up the empty mocha cup she had left on the console the morning before last, and ambled out into the house's kitchen.

## Onboard the *ArchAngel*, General Reynolds's Office

Giles strode through the open door to the General's office suite and glanced around. There was no one in the main room, but he could hear movement in the office area.

He took another step inside and hesitated.

A moment later, Lance appeared, his boyishly young face the same as it had been when Giles was a kid.

"Hello, G-man!" Lance greeted him, walking into the room and shaking his hand before embracing him warmly.

"Hello, Uncle Lance. How are you?" Giles returned the one-armed hug and the manly patting on the back.

"Good. Goooood," the General responded, releasing Giles from his hug. "How are you, young man?" he asked, looking Giles up and down. "I hear you had a close call out in the Terroc regions a few months back?"

Giles nodded, his eyes looking suddenly old as he scratched at the back of his head. "Yeah. Yeah, it was a rough time. I was lucky, though." He paused, bringing his eyes up to meet the General's. "And I appreciate you pulling a few strings to get me out of there. Really. Thank you, General."

Lance waved a hand, and put his arm around the boy. "Don't mention it. I'd never hear the last of it from your father if I'd left you there to rot." He walked Giles over to the sofas and offered him a seat. Then he headed over to the tray of drinks.

Giles bobbed his head as he sat down. "I heard that my mother said to leave me there and let me learn my lesson about wandering into hostile territories." He wore a half-smile, and his eyes seemed tinged with sadness.

The General turned around, having poured a Scotch, and walked over to hand it to him. "You know that's just her way of saying she wished you'd stay home and out of trouble."

Giles took the drink, and nodded his thanks. "Yeah, I guess," he agreed. "I know she means well."

The General smiled. "Barb is from a different age. Survival was all-important back then - before the nanocytes, and so on. People had to be more careful. More wary. Plus, you know what she went through."

Giles nodded. He knew the General made sense, and yet...

"I dunno. I always feel like she's judging my lifestyle choice."

The General poured himself a Scotch and turned around, a big grin on his face. "My boy, *everyone* is judging your lifestyle choice!"

The two of them laughed, breaking the seriousness of the conversation. They raised their glasses and took their first sip.

"Good to see you, you nomadic hippie-ghost hunter," the General told the middle-aged-looking professor.

Giles smiled. "You too, Uncle."

The General regarded the man in front of him and shook his head, smiling. "You know, I still don't understand why you had your nanocytes reprogrammed to make you look old," he remarked quietly, as if musing to himself.

Giles grinned back at Lance. "I don't look old. I look forty!"

The General nodded. "Yes. Forty. I never did understand that."

Giles shrugged and leaned back in the sofa, resting his tumbler on his leg and holding it with two fingers.

"Well, my father sits behind a desk, sheltered in this palace of a ship. He never need interact with anyone from a culture he doesn't understand. And outside the Etheric Empire, age counts for something; it's sacred. It's respected."

Lance looked genuinely curious, his jesting subsided. "You mean you find your research easier when people don't assume you're a kid?"

Giles nodded once. "Precisely what I'm saying."

Lance chuckled, pulled a fresh cigar out of his pocket, and popped it in his mouth before sitting on the other sofa.

Giles turned in his seat to face him. "Have you seen my father recently?" he asked.

The General's tone became almost chatty. "Yes, he and Barb were around for supper the other week. He's embarrassed about his golf swing, and your mother is poking at all kinds of projects and investigations we have ongoing in the various systems."

"Ha!" Giles exclaimed. "Just like Mom; she never could leave anything alone."

Lance nodded, almost solemnly. "Yes. And sometimes we have to reel her back in to keep her safe. And keep her from starting a galactic war... but it's all par for the course."

Giles shook his head. "She's such a hypocrite!" he mused, looking into his Scotch glass. "Well, I hope she's not giving you too much trouble."

The General chuckled. "Not at all, chap. I'm glad we have her on the team," he assured him.

Giles's curiosity was burning, and he was dying to find out what he'd missed since he was last in with the General for a briefing.

"So I'm assuming you didn't have ADAM bring me up here just to do small talk?"

The General took a deep breath, his demeanor shifting again into work-mode. "No. You guessed right," he confirmed. "Of course, I'd like the usual update on your travels and investigations; but first," he got up and moved over to the holo in the middle of the side wall, "I wonder if I can ask for your expert opinion on something?"

Giles shuffled forward onto the edge of his seat, placing the Scotch glass on the glass coffee table in front of him.

"Of course, sir."

Lance smiled at the 'sir' part. Having watched Giles grow up on this very ship, and now having the man in front of him calling him 'sir' as soon as they got down to business – he couldn't help but be amused at the cultural norms.

"ADAM, could you put what we know about Molly's situation onscreen, please?"

The holoscreen opened out as an array of several screens. Lance pulled one out and pushed it over for Giles to see.

"These are the neuroscans we took when she was in the pod doc. She was brought to us after being shot."

Giles looked up, a little concerned. "And this is the operative you recruited for Gaitune?" he confirmed.

Lance nodded. "Yes. The same one."

Giles studied the screen and flicked through the time-lapse layers, watching the repair happen. Then he quickly flicked through to the final scan. His eyes widened a little, and his head moved backward in shock.

"You notice something?" Lance asked.

Giles glanced up, and then returned his eyes to the scan. "Er. Yes..." He hesitated, a little distracted.

Lance waited.

Giles finally looked up, and turned the holo so Lance could view it, too.

"See this area of the brain here?" he pointed at an area in the middle of the head. Then, using his thumb and forefinger, he pulled the image out, and expanded it into a three dimensional representation. He turned the image of the color-mapped brain while Lance watched carefully. Giles expanded it again, and pointed into the temporal lobe area.

"This area here is more active than in a normal human. It's associated with various psychic phenomena, ranging from the Seers of the Sandrahine, through to the Shamans of Earth – even the Ascending Estarians register this area of their brains as being more active than in normal brains."

He sat back, allowing the General to study the scan data

longer. Lance didn't look up. "So you're telling me that her physiology is changed? As a result of the pod doc?"

Giles pursed his lips. "I can't tell from this if it is a result of the pod doc or not. I mean, her whole brain was shut down at the beginning of the scan."

He flipped the time code back to the beginning to show Lance the contrast. "This means that we can't know if she already had the activity in her brain when it was functioning normally, or whether it was a result of the enhancement that the pod doc created. Though if that were the case, I suspect we would have seen more instances of it before now..." His voice faded a little as he considered something else.

Lance noticed Giles was thinking, and looked over at him before perching on the seat next to him.

Giles realized the General was waiting for him to explain.

"I think the other thing to consider," he said, looking over at Lance, "is that perhaps death was the thing that triggered this awakening of activity." Giles shrugged, showing he wasn't attached to the idea. "Of course," he tipped his head slightly as he explained, "there are countless documented cases of people coming back with enhanced cognitive function in certain areas - especially since our technology is becoming more effective at restoring brain activity within the death window."

Lance glanced at him, and then sat back in the sofa, contemplating. "Anything else?" he asked.

Giles flicked back through the scan, and then honed in on one time slice to view the construction of the neurons.

"Her brain scans show that her neurons are different, too. Might have something to do with her heightened intelligence," Giles paused, and closed down the scans. He turned and looked at Lance again.

"...but also may be why the AI selected her."

The General took the cigar from his mouth and rubbed his face, now leaning with his elbows on his knees.

Giles studied him carefully. "What is it?" he asked, being careful not to overstep a mark.

Lance shook his head gently. "Well, if she does have Etheric abilities, which is what your old friend Arlene is suggesting, what does this mean?"

Giles brightened. "Ah, you've spoken to Arlene?"

The General nodded. "Yes," he smiled dryly. "She sends her best – and asked when you were going to get around to publishing that paper."

Giles blushed, and looked away uncomfortably.

Lance caught that there was more of a story there, and decided it was something to tease him about later over dinner. He stayed on-task. "She took the girl out on some kind of Estarian Vision Quest. Does that mean anything to you?"

Giles nodded excitedly. "Ooh. Yes. Yes it does." He stood up as if he couldn't contain his enthusiasm. "What she's probably seen is her shift into the different realms; which makes sense, from her physiology." He pointed back at the open holoscreens and then started pacing, animating his hands in front of him as he talked.

"I'm wondering... You're sure Arlene mentioned she touched the Etheric?"

Lance nodded. "Yep. It's the kind of thing one tends to remember."

Giles shook his head, a look of amazement on his face. "Well," he sighed brightly. "Guess I should have a conversation with Arlene," he decided.

Lance nodded absently. "Of course. She's on Gaitune, still. You can connect with her through ADAM."

Giles brought his enthused anthropological mystical mind back to Lance, recognizing that he was still perplexed by the details they'd been discussing.

"You're worried about what this means for The Empire?" he guessed.

Lance nodded. "I am. If it's induced by the pod doc, or by the near-death, then it looks like Bethany Anne, Michael, and the Five aren't the only ones who will have the advantage of the Etheric." Lance seemed to pull himself back from his thoughts. "Of course, everything we've discussed is classified," he remarked gruffly, chewing on his cigar.

Giles nodded. "Of course, sir."

Lance stood up and walked over to the drinks tray, topping off his own tumbler, and then reaching for Giles's, which was almost untouched on the coffee table. He topped his off a little, anyway.

"Do some digging for me? I want to know everything there is to know - including what the likely causes are, and also if it can be weaponized."

Lance turned his attention back to Giles's face just in time to see him react in pacifist, academic horror at his last word.

"Don't look at me like that," he said, taking another swig of Scotch. "You know that's exactly the question Bethany Anne would be asking if she were here."

Giles lowered his eyes. "Yes, of course." He took a deep breath and wandered back to the sofa to drink some of his Scotch before Lance would whisk him off to the officers' mess for dinner.

"I knew a hundred years of playing in cultural anthropology funded by the Empire was going to require some kind of payback, eventually," Giles grinned carefully, trying not to spill his Scotch through his smile as he took another sip.

Lance caught his eye and smiled back, raising his glass. Giles wasn't positive, but he could have sworn he saw the General wink at him.

CHAPTER FIFTEEN

**On board *The Empress*, Gaitune-67, Hangar Deck**

Paige and Maya stood in *The Empress*'s medical bay, watching Pieter and Brock steer Crash into one of the med docks. Thanks to Emma showing them the troop entrance into the ship from the bottom, they didn't have to try and maneuver him through the narrow passageway and into the upstairs of the craft.

"How are they going to get him inside?" Maya whispered to Paige as they watched them line him up with the nearest dock.

Sean overheard them as he strode back in. "We lift the stretcher in, and then deactivate it and leave it there for when we want to help him back out," he told them.

Pieter and Brock heard, and set about doing just that.

As they were lifting him in, Molly and Joel wandered in. Molly's eyes were red and puffy, and Joel's t-shirt was wet on the shoulder. It was clear to Paige that he had been taking care of her, and rather than make a thing of her crying, she just waved and smiled a little.

Molly waved back before heading over to the med dock to see Crash. "How's he doing?" she asked Sean.

Crash had been lowered into the coffin-like dock, and Sean

pressed a few buttons on the holo panel. "How about we ask Emma what her diagnosis is?"

Molly nodded and watched as the field powered up and started scanning the body inside.

Emma's voice came from the dock panel. "Crash is operating within acceptable parameters: heart rate, normal for resting; blood pressure normal; brain activity... compromised; slight concussion, and a lack of consciousness. One laceration, one inch long; slight swelling around the brain. Implementing brain-swell-reduction and repair.

The plane of light that had been scanning Crash's body swept deftly up to his head, and started moving slowly around the affected area. It glided slowly back and forth along a section marked between his nose and eyes – back and forth, back and forth.

Paige whispered to Maya. "It looks like it's 3D-printing his brain back together."

Maya nodded without taking her eyes from the pod.

Joel noticed that Molly was holding her breath as she watched.

*Was this what it was like when I was in the pod doc?*

**Not really. I mean, I can't tell because I was inside you, but from the repair that I noticed, it wasn't in one area at a time – it was more an all-over, gradual improvement. But that was different technology, that tapped into your DNA. I suspect here we're looking at some form of growth stim-ulation.**

*Hmm. I'd be interested to find out more about it. Can you find out from Emma later?*

**Sure. Us AIs love to have a chinwag over interesting topics.**

*You're kidding?*

**No. I'm serious. It's nice to have friends of my own species.**

Molly smiled to herself, hugging her arms around her body, comforted that Oz was happy and making actual friends.

Emma's voice interrupted over the dock speaker. "Brain repair complete. Shall I wake the subject?"

Sean pressed a button, and had a quick look at a few charts that Molly couldn't quite make out from over his shoulder.

"Yes, please, Emma. Wake *Crash* up, if you would."

**Haha. She got rumbled for calling him a 'subject'! I'm totally LOL-ing over here.**

*Oz...*

Molly shook her head, smiling to herself, trying not to look like the crazy person in the room.

Pieter and Brock were looking hopeful. Almost relieved.

A moment later, Crash's breathing became more pronounced, and his eyes flickered, and then opened. He took some proper breaths, and started to look around, bewildered.

Molly put her hand to her chest and stepped back, breathing deeper herself. In her case, it was from relief.

Brock moved closer to Crash and put his hand on Crash's chest. He was talking with him quietly, explaining that he had a fall, and that they were in a medical bay on *The Empress*.

Molly backed off a little more and moved toward the door, followed by Joel. The two quietly stepped out into the corridor, leaving the rest of the team to welcome Crash back into the world.

Molly ran her fingers through her hair, pulling it out of her face and holding her head, as she took a few paces.

"Hey," Joel called after her. "You doing okay?" he asked.

She turned and smiled a brave smile. "Yeah. Glad he's okay. That was... intense."

Joel nodded. "Okay. Let's get you some food and rack time. And I want to hear more about what happened out there. Something tells me this realm thing hasn't been resolved, if you rushed back here."

Molly bobbed her head from side to side indicating a, 'yes and no'. She sighed.

"Yeah. I guess not; but I have made progress."

She started telling him about the last two days' events, as they left the ship and made their way back up to the safe house.

## Gaitune-67, Base conference room

Two days later, things seemed to have returned to normal.

Crash, completely healed, was back to practicing on *The Empress* with Emma, and everyone else was working on their respective tasks. By the afternoon, Molly had called a team meeting to decide on their plan of action.

The team was tired from their preparations; Brock seemed to be functioning mostly on mocha, and even Pieter was a little wired, suggesting they'd been burning the midnight oil together to get the tech up to spec.

Despite Crash's near miss, he was also looking fatigued – although Oz had reported back to Molly that Emma was implementing a much stricter rest routine for him. Paige and Maya weren't looking their usual well-manicured selves, and had resorted to walking around the base in sweat gear and overalls, rather than their usual haute couture. Paige had even taken to pulling her hair up to save on maintenance.

The only ones who truly looked bright-eyed and battle-ready were Jack, Sean, and Joel. Molly suspected that it had something to do with their experience with mission prep, and being able to keep themselves in peak condition in the run up to a mission. Life in the military forces one to be ready for anything, whether it's moving out at a moment's notice, or, indeed, sitting around waiting, and *then* having to move at a moment's notice.

Molly had been off mocha for a while now, still unable to keep it down, and, in coming to terms with that, she was finding a new rhythm.

Molly convened the meeting – her focus on all the moving

parts, preventing her from being distracted by the extraneous details of social interaction.

"Okay, folks, let's get to it," she announced, and the hub-bub settled in seconds.

"The overall picture is this," she told them. "In less than 48 hours from now, we need to be heading back to the planet, Kurilia. Once there, we will implement our plan to ensure that all secret military capabilities are permanently disabled. This is a precision mission," she explained.

She glanced around at the attentive faces of her teammates.

"Not only that," she continued, "but Oz's team will implant the worm that will monitor their whole operation from the moment we leave the planet. Paige's team will deploy what we're calling a 'disclosure campaign.'"

Molly paused, seeming to speak with Oz for a moment. Then she brought her attention back to the team.

"I know this last point is a little... unconventional, but, having discussed it with ADAM, we're looking to try something new; something that will hopefully prevent a backlash down the line. We haven't got time to go into the whys and wherefores, but, in essence, the Federation is hoping that the Zhyn will eventually become allies. The less we give them to be resentful about, the better. Maya will explain more when we get to this item."

*Oz, can you pull up the mission summary so everyone can track the key elements?*

**On it.**

"Right let's dig into the details," she said, indicating to the hologram opening from the center of the table.

The screen unfolded to reveal a bulleted list of the mission objectives:

> Disable the secret military bases

> Deploy software worm to take comms and weapons offline - permanently

> Deploy media campaign to reveal the secret agenda to the populace

Sean whistled quietly through his teeth. "That's a lot to accomplish with just our little team," he said quietly.

Molly heard, and nodded. "That's why we need a super-enhanced cyborg on our side." There was a chuckle through the room. "I don't suppose you've seen one anywhere?" There was more laughter.

Joel pushed his chair back and pretended to look under the table. Pieter was laughing silently, and started gently tapping the table in amusement with the flat of his hand. The mood lightened despite the complexity of the mission ahead of them.

Sean nodded, turning a little pink, and took the shit that was being handed to him.

Molly continued, still smiling. "We also have lots of other advantages we can leverage. As you'll see." She looked pointedly at Sean, wanting to be able to continue with the briefing.

He had his hands flat on the table in front of him, and, getting the point of her stare, he raised his hands slightly, conceding the floor to her.

Molly continued. "Okay. Disabling the military capabilities. This has several phases to it. Joel, this is your piece of the op; wanna explain the phases?"

Joel pushed back his seat and stood up, bringing up a map of the planet, and all the bases that were their targets.

"Sure," he said, as he prepared his screens.

"Our goal," he told them, "is to take out *only* the secret military bases. Not the official, legitimate ones."

He paused, making sure everyone understood that. Then he continued.

"At each of the secret bases, we will take out the weapons systems, the communications systems, and their power. Nothing else. We're trying to do this with minimal casualties, and the last thing we want is to get stuck in a firefight. We want to be in and out."

"To that end," he continued, "let's look at the potential issues – because there is no getting around having to put boots on the ground, with this one."

He put his hands up in front of him, and used the movement to zoom in on the holomap of two targets that were fairly close together. "Oz's team has got the comms and weapons covered. Most of our ground targets can be addressed using nanodrones, which Oz will also remotely deploy and target. But," he paused, flicking the map over to another layer, "there are a few targets where we will need to physically deploy charges."

He indicated to the two he'd zoomed in on, and then showed them a third on the southern hemisphere. He looked around the room, and then down at Molly sitting on his right-hand side.

"These are the three targets. Two of them are close to their skylifts. The other one is just over a mile's hike from the first target."

Maya put her hand up. "What *are* those targets, though?" she asked.

Joel zoomed in again, showing their outline more clearly. "They're generators. We know this from Oz's intel. What we can't see, is where to blow them up – because they're shielded with Faraday cages and forcefields. We need to be on the ground to figure it out, and then set the charges in the weak spots. Too much firepower in this area could cause all kinds of destruction. We need to be precise…"

His voice trailed off as he wondered how much detail to share with them. He shook his head minutely, and decided to move on with the intel they needed to know.

"On the plus side, Brock has come up with a way to detonate all the charges remotely. So as long as we can get in and out, Oz can take care of the rest."

Joel returned to his seat and checked some notes on his holo.

"To this end, we'll deploy two teams. Team one: Sean and Molly. They will take the first two targets. Team two is myself and Jack. We will be dropped on the southern hemisphere skylift to take out the third target. With a bit of luck, we can each get back to our respective skylifts before all hell breaks loose."

He looked matter-of-fact, but Paige was paying close attention to his micro expressions. There was something he was concerned about in his last statement. She made a mental note to find out what was bothering him.

Joel continued with his briefing.

"This brings us on to Oz's part of the mission. Oz will be responsible for the detonation – which he'll hopefully hold off on until we're back at the top of the skylift, and ready to be extracted. Oz, you want to take the next section?"

Oz's voice cracked over the comm system. "Sure. Yes, I'll be waiting to detonate everything after you've been extracted. However, there are other layers of the assault that can't wait. Pieter, Paige, Maya, and myself have been working on a number of things to take out the various systems. Pieter and I are going to be able to take out their weapons permanently, by corrupting every last line of code running in those secret bases. Not only that, but we have a fireworks display of technological destruction planned, where we can overheat critical points of hardware, too. There will be nothing left of these bases that they can use."

Sean grinned, nodding his head in appreciation of the prospect of technological carnage. Pieter glanced over, his eyes catching the movement, and, despite his fatigue, he grinned back.

"Then all that leaves is the PR campaign," Oz added. "Maya?"

Maya sat up straighter and began to explain her part of the operation.

"The public communication campaign will be broadcast on all civilian channels, reeducating the population as to what is really happening on their planet. It will expose the secret bases that have been built in contravention to the Jah-Dune Accord.

It will also explain why this is a problem, in terms of inter-world affairs, and how their Emperor is effectively putting a target on them by pursuing this aggressive secret-armament strategy."

Molly picked up the explanation. "The reason for doing this is to stop the military from hacking straight into civilian resources to try and rearm, and re-engage," she told them. "If the public is aware of the issue, they will have a revolt on their hands."

She got up and started pacing the long side of the conference room.

"According to ADAM, there is history to suggest that where the government has betrayed the wishes of the people, there have been dire consequences. Fortunately, this means the people will likely be on our side. They want peace, but what is happening right now is that their military is going rogue because they have had so little accountability."

Molly glanced back at the bulleted list still on display at the center of the large conference table.

"Okay. We've covered all the main elements. Anything else?"

Brock waved his hand. "Yeah. I think it's worth mentioning that we've adapted some of the gear to make it less kill-y and more disable-y."

Molly nodded. "Yes, of course. Since our aim is only to disable the secret military bases, I felt that some of the weaponry we had for the ground operation was a little... brutal. Brock has been working to adapt some of it."

She paused, looking at Sean, knowing his view on the subject. "Of course, if we *need* to kill, that setting is still available on the blasters; but where we can avoid it, we now have the option. Brock," she turned back to him, "if you can fit in a quick training session with the folks who will be carrying them on the ride in, that would be great."

Brock nodded.

Molly looked around the table. "Anything else?"

There were lots of headshakes and mumbles. Molly concluded the meeting.

"Okay, great. Between now and departure, I want everyone to get as much rest as they can. We all need to be at our best, and that means not over-training, and not pushing ourselves to exhaustion."

She deliberately avoided eye contact with Crash so that he didn't feel like he was being singled out.

"Okay, folks. Dismissed," she concluded.

The antigrav chairs were pushed out as the team got up and milled around, either talking or moving on to the next thing they needed to get done. Gradually, the room emptied out under an air of focus, and a sense of "getting shit done."

# CHAPTER SIXTEEN

**On Board *The Empress*, Koin Star System**

"This is your captain speaking." Crash's voice came over the ship-wide intercom.

"We are fast-approaching our destination. The weather on Kurilia is sunny, with a light westernly breeze, and a 90% chance of anarchy. We will shortly commence our descent to the skylifts, where you will be taken to the surface, free of charge, by our sponsors, Kurilia Media. On arrival, please keep your hands and arms inside the ship, and do not feed the animals. Make sure your weapons are fully charged, and remember: have a nice day."

Jack, Sean, and Joel were already in the basement, ready to deploy the trapdoor and drop frame. Kitted up, they waited patiently to pick up the somewhat cumbersome Zhyn blasters. They all smiled, amused at Crash's announcement, and all secretly thinking how glad they were that he was okay.

Molly heard the announcement, too, and she started to get her stuff together from her seat in the back of the cabin. She'd been practicing her meditation and breathing, and finding herself more in control.

*Okay. This is it, Oz.*

**We've got this; Pieter is almost ready to deploy the worm. We'll be good as soon as we're within orbit.**

*Great.*

Molly stopped suddenly, and, though she'd been starting to get up, she quickly sat back down.

**Everything all right?**

*Er. I'm not sure. I...*

**Molly, your adrenaline has spiked and you're releasing excess cortisol.**

*You mean I'm experiencing fear?*

**It seems so. What did you just start thinking about?**

*Nothing new. I was just thinking about putting the rest of my gear on. But then...*

She paused, and then looked around the cabin.

**What is it?**

*I just had a sense of Paige.*

**Paige?**

*Yeah. So, you know how I told you about my time out on the asteroid, and how Arlene had me tune into each person and read them?*

**Yes.**

*Well, I think I just accidentally read Paige.*

**Oops.**

*Yeah. She's nervous, thinking about all the things that could go wrong.*

**That can't be good.**

*Hmm. Okay, lemme see if I can close it down.*

Molly got up, and took herself down to the basement. She descended the steps, careful to keep herself grounded and present, as Arlene had showed her.

**Molly? What is it now?**

*I'm picking up on the others. Sean, Jack, and Joel. I can feel each of them clearly.*

**Can you close it down?**

*I'm not sure. I'm going to try.*

Molly stood still where she was for a minute, breathing and trying to center herself.

*Oz. It's not working.*

**Why not?**

Molly shook her head and tried to ignore the feelings that were rushing through her system. She entered the room to see the guys opening the trapdoor.

*I dunno. Shit, I need to get ready.*

"Cutting it a little fine, Mollz," Sean said in battle-jest. She could feel his edginess coming out, behind his words. This was how he coped with the pressure and the adrenaline. She suspected it also helped with the camaraderie; she felt it a little in the other warriors assembled, too.

"Yeah," she agreed, walking over to where the rest of her body armor was. She quickly got it on, and checked her holsters. Finally, she found her wooden baton, and stuffed it down between the holsters and vest on her back.

*Can still feel them all.*

**You doing okay?**

*Yeah. Just feeling a little icky, and like my energy is being depleted by it.*

**Think you should tell someone?**

*Right, and give Sean another reason to think that I'm a bad leader? I don't think so.*

**He doesn't think that.**

*No, but he does think that I'm physically weak, and probably shouldn't be on this mission until I've got this realm shit sorted out.*

**How do you know that?**

*I can feel it from him.*

**Are you sure? I mean, projection, eh?**

*Nope. I'm not sure. I can never be sure. But since the Vision Quest, I'm learning to trust my gut.*

**Okay. As long as your gut doesn't get you thinking things that aren't there.**

*Yeah. Anyway – time to focus.*

Molly walked over to the arms rack on the far side of the room, and pulled one of the blasters off of it. She checked the settings: safety, on, off, and the toggle for kill versus stun.

The others were reaching over to grab theirs, too.

Sean reached past her and smiled. "You got your charges?" he asked.

Molly nodded and patted the long pocket in her suit trousers. "Yep. All set."

"Good," he smiled.

The team got ready to take themselves down.

Brock walked in just as Emma clicked onto the local holopanel. "We're on the final approach. Just a few more minutes, and we'll be passing by the first drop point."

Molly and Sean made eye contact. "That'll be us," she said, wondering whether she should let him know what was going on with her.

Joel was hanging onto the frame, which had already come down to help their descent.

"Look," he said, addressing the drop team. "Don't take any unnecessary risks down there. This is a simple in and out. If you can't reach your target, we'll have to do what we can with the nanodrones, and hope for the best. Your mantra for today is to make sure that you're around to fight another day."

He paused, looking at each of them in turn. "Understood?"

They each nodded.

"Okay, good. Molly, Sean, you're up."


**On Board *The Empress*, Main cabin**

Paige and Maya moved a few seats closer to where Pieter was working. Paige noticed he was hyper-focused as he worked to link into the base protocol.

Oz's voice connected with the auditory system in the cabin. "Okay, they're all clear of the ship. Time to deploy the worm."

Pieter nodded. "Okay. Just one more minute, and we'll be through their firewall."

Paige and Maya watched intently as he worked. A moment later, Pieter's expression changed, and his shoulders dropped a little. "Okay, we're in. Oz, it's all yours."

"Thank you, Pieter" Oz replied. "Worm deploying."

Maya turned to Paige. "Okay, so as soon as the broadcasts are released, they will start running on all the major civilian and military channels. Oz and Pieter are going to hack that separately, though."

Paige frowned. "Why's that?"

Maya lowered her voice so as not to distract Pieter and Oz from what they were doing. "Something about the secret bases using not only an isolated computer system, but also a different type of code. Hacking that isn't the same as hacking the civilian network; but they seem sure that getting into the civilian network won't be nearly as difficult." She glanced back at Pieter, who was watching his screen intently.

"Everything okay, Pieter?" Paige asked, noticing that he was just watching the screen and not typing anything now.

Pieter nodded. "Yeah. It will be. It's looking like this worm is going to take at least forty minutes to be fully deployed, though..."

Paige frowned. "Is that longer than you were hoping?" she asked.

Pieter looked over at them, his face gaunt and tired. "A little." He turned his attention back to the screen. "It should be okay, though," he added quietly.

Paige nodded. "And then you upload the campaign?"

Pieter kept his eyes on the holo this time. "Yeah. That's the plan. All being well..."

He ran a hand over his face, barely peeling his eyes from his screen for a moment, and then returned to willing the worm to deploy faster.

### Planet Kurilia, Northern Hemisphere drop

Molly and Sean peered out of the skylift doors at the clearing around the lift. Blasters at the ready, and eyes and ears on high alert for any signs of movement in the tree line, Sean swung out first. He swept his weapon back and forth, following his line of sight, making sure that they weren't about to be ambushed.

Molly carefully ventured out after him; diligently, so as not to allow the blaster end of her weapon to cross his location.

Sean took a moment, and then relaxed a little while still keeping his senses trained in ops mode. "This is where you came down before? With Joel and Jack?" he asked.

Molly came up beside him, lowering her blaster a little. "Yes, that's right. Feels a little like déjà vu, actually."

Sean glanced down at her. "You sure you're okay with all this?"

Molly frowned. "How do you mean?"

Sean looked back at the tree line, then down at his holo to check their location. "Well, you know – with all the realm stuff. I mean, are you sure you're ready?"

*Here we go...* Molly thought.

She felt herself getting a little irritated, and tried not to show it. "Yes. I'm fine. I learned a lot with Arlene, and I have more control." She glanced around getting her bearings. "First target is this way," she indicated, spinning around and heading around the other side of the skylift.

Sean closed his holo, having checked and agreed with her conclusion. "Okay, lead the way," he said. The tone of his voice seemed to suggest an undercurrent of 'on your head be it,' but Molly chose to ignore it.

**How you feeling now?**

*Fine.*

**Fine?**

*Well, yeah. Sean... you know. But I'm doing okay. Feels lighter, now that it's just Sean in my space.*

**Okay. That's... something.**

Oz paused a moment, but Molly could feel him humming in her head.

*What is it?*

**Don't you think you should have mentioned it to him? About how you're feeling people in your space, and it's taking you off your game?**

*What, and give him the satisfaction of being right?*

**Well, operationally, he should at least be aware. What if something happens?**

*Well, then, I'll deal. I don't want him thinking he needs to babysit me. We get enough of that from him anyway, just cuz we're not super-enhanced starship frikkin' troopers.*

**True. And yet...**

*Okay. Noted. I'll see. If we are in and out as we planned, it won't be an issue.*

Oz was present and silent.

*What?* Molly pressed again.

**Well, I'm starting to learn that no plan survives contact with the enemy.**

Molly nodded. Oz was right. She should probably mention something to him. She sighed.

*Okay. I'll say something if it becomes relevant.*

Sean had trudged on down a single tracked path in the lush undergrowth. Molly had to work to keep up with him; she found herself breathing a little heavier than she normally would.

*Oz, have I just become unfit with all this sitting around and meditating?*

Oz ran a calculation.

**It seems your average weekly activity has declined by 51% since you started down that course.**

*Hmm. I'm sure Sean said that the nanocytes would mean I wouldn't need to train as hard to be twice as fit...*

**Maybe he lied.**

Molly chuckled out loud.

Sean turned his head to call back to her quietly. "Having fun back there?"

"A little." Molly replied. "Though it wouldn't kill you to slow down a bit!"

"HA! Struggling to keep up, eh? We'll have to fix that, next training session. Come on, the sooner we get these charges set, the sooner we can get the hell out of here."

"I couldn't agree more," Molly replied, picking up her pace to catch up as they made their way through the undergrowth, carrying their not-so-light blasters in the temperate climate.


## Planet Kurilia, Koin Star System, Zhyn Empire, Control Room of PrimeBase

"Sir, it looks like our security protocols have been compromised again. Something is happening to our systems; they're not responding."

Commander Thatle stepped over to view the details on the console.

"Can you lock it down?" he asked the console operator.

"Tech is working on it," the lieutenant reported back, "but it looks like the mainframe has already been taken over. They have a few things they can try in order to isolate the intrusion, and we're taking the backup servers offline now."

Thatle contemplated the intel for a moment. "Fine," he said finally. "Keep me posted. Let me know as soon as you hear anything else."

"Yes, sir."

The commander moved to another console, and addressed the lieutenant monitoring the cameras. "We've been breached again," Thatle told him, his large presence behind the slightly built Zhyn unnerving the subordinate. "Probably the same intruder as last time," he continued. "Tell me, have we got a visual on anyone coming onto the surface in the last six hours? Also do a search in the vicinity around each base, in case the perpetrators are the same one."

The lieutenant stopped what he was doing to carry out the order immediately. "Facial rec engaging, sir," he confirmed, keen to impress.

The commander stood patiently behind the lieutenant, watching the screen flick through the commands and combinations. He had considered that these humans might return, and had already planned out his strategy for dealing with them.

Thatle composed himself for a moment, looking off into the distance; his attention so focused in his mind's eye, he barely saw the buzz of activity in his control room.

"Sir," the lieutenant interrupted his thoughts. "We have visuals on four intruders. Two near here, and two on the other side of the planet at the Darfine Base."

Thatle checked the output on the console, and confirmed the coordinates of the flagged location. "Very good, lieutenant," he said when he was satisfied. "Thank you."

The operator of the console shifted in his seat to try and look at his commander. "Your orders, sir?" he inquired.

The commander looked off across the control room, thinking. "Send in troops. Fast and agile. We want to capture them alive to find out what they've been doing to our systems. But if that's not possible, our secondary intention is to neutralize the threat."

"Aye, sir," the lieutenant acknowledged.

The order was relayed to the communications officer on the next console, who then issued the order to the ground squadron.

The commander turned on his heels and headed straight to

his office to make the call up the chain. He felt a bubble of tension rising in his chest; he was secretly anxious, but also proud that he was ready for this second attack. He would have this problem handled in no time.

As he strode through the consoles of the command center, the high-alert alarm sounded throughout, turning the room dark with red flashing lights. The sound penetrated every eardrum, disturbing normal concentration and instilling a sense of urgency. The commander retained an air of calm, as he stepped into his office and allowed the door to slide shut behind him. Immediately the noise was cut out, leaving an empty silence.

In the quiet, he gradually became aware of the sound of his own breathing, his own heart rate pulsing through his body, and the sound of his own footsteps on the floor as he walked over to his console to make the call.

He clicked on his communication device. "Vice High Marshall Davon," he instructed the computer. The call connected.

"Sir, I have news of the intruders," Thatle reported.

He paused while Davon spoke on the other end of the call.

"Yes, sir. They have touched down on foot in two points we've located so far. I have troops on their way to pick them up."

He waited for the order from Davon, listening intently, hoping that his plan was going to meet with approval.

His shoulders dropped as he relaxed, hearing Davon's words. He responded graciously. "Yes, sir. Understood. Extreme prejudice."

There was another pause as he listened, and then, "Yes, of course. The tech team is working on it now. I'll let you know as soon as we hear."

The call ended, and the commander returned to the silence of his office to contemplate his next move in thwarting the attack.

CHAPTER SEVENTEEN

**On Board** *The Empress*, **Main cabin**

Oz's voice reported through Pieter's implant. "We have a problem."

Pieter stopped what he was typing. "What kind of problem?" he asked.

"Both teams have been detected," Oz told him. "The Zhyn command has issued an order to put troops at each location. I'm going to warn Molly and Joel."

Pieter put both hands to his face and rubbed his forehead fast. "Shit," he whispered in frustration. "What else can we do?"

Oz remained calm. "See if you can take out the communications so they can't deploy their troops. Then see if there is some way to keep from tracking them. It looks like they used facial recognition and cameras to identify them; if any of those systems are offline, or unable to reference the database, then we might be able to buy them some time."

Pieter's fingers were back on his holo keyboard. "Okay. I'm on it," he said, his skin turning a shade of deeper gray with stress.

Oz explained his next move through Pieter's audio implant while he worked. "I'm going to try and guide Molly and Joel to

171

steer clear, but if we take their systems offline, we'll be blind, too - to their troops, and their location."

Pieter paused his typing. "I'm not sure we have a choice," he said, tilting his head back and thinking it through. "All of them have local maps, and know how to handle themselves. I think our best option is to take the cameras, and whatever else they're using, offline to cripple the advance of the troops."

"Agreed," confirmed Oz. "I'll let them know what's happening."

Oz disappeared from the audio connection, and Pieter got to his suddenly-urgent task.

### Planet Kurilia, Northern Hemisphere

"Okay, that's one down, one to go," Sean announced as he placed the last charge on the external forcefield of their first target generator.

"Good job!" Molly called, turning to check their surroundings again. She had started to feel faint.

Sean noticed she was sweating and had gone a little pale. "You okay?" he asked.

Molly nodded. "Yeah, just a little – "

**Molly?**

*Yes?*

**We have an issue. They know you're there; they have your locations.**

Molly looked over at Sean, her eyes wide and creased at the edges with anxiety.

"We have company on the way," she relayed to him.

Sean looked a little more alert. "How long, and what direction?"

Oz responded through both their audio implants. "They're coming from The South Southwest direction. You've probably got five minutes before they reach your location."

Sean looked confused. "How did they find us?"

As they started moving in the opposite direction, Oz's voice informed them, "Facial recognition, from when Molly was down here before. Then they're assuming the target you're going after. I don't think they have another way of tracking you."

Molly nodded. "That means we can probably avoid them, if we take a different route to our next target; if we move unpredictably."

Sean glanced over at her as they stomped quickly though the undergrowth. "That sounds like a plan, though it will mean more time here on the planet."

"Sucks to be us," agreed Molly.

Sean checked his holomap and looked back at the generator they were leaving behind.

"I guess," added Molly, "if we go a couple of miles that way and then double back from the other angle, we'll miss them, and still be able to hit the next target in the minimum time."

"Agreed," Sean grunted, closing the holomap.

*Have you alerted Joel and Jack?*

**Yes, doing it now.**

*Okay, make sure they have a plan for extraction – no being heroes!*

**Yes, Joel is well aware of that. They're still en route to their first target.**

*Okay. Keep me in the loop. Thanks, Oz.*

**Of course.**

## Planet Kurilia, Koin Star System, Zhyn Empire, Control Room of PrimeBase

The commander stood behind the lieutenant at the comms console.

"What do we know?" he asked.

The lieutenant didn't take his eyes from the screen, but reported back swiftly. "We know they hacked into our communications systems and pulled off intel; presumably to know where our people were coming from, in order to aid their people on the ground."

He paused, flicking a few switches on the holos in front of him. "We've since moved to quantum, so we're untraceable until they get eyes on us."

The commander nodded his head, listening carefully. "Anything else?"

"Yes," the lieutenant continued, "our tactical department had a theory that they were going after the main three, and, tracking their movements thus far, that looks accurate. We deployed troops to intercept them at the targets; we'll have them either neutralized or in our custody in a matter of minutes, sir."

"Good," Thatle replied gruffly. "Let me know as soon as that happens."

"Yes, sir."

Thatle stepped away from the communications station and headed back to the liaison for the technical department. He stood off to the side as the captain finished relaying current messages between the various teams working planet-wide to combat the intrusion.

Eventually, he had the captain's full attention. "Any progress?" Thatle asked.

The captain tried to maintain an emotionless expression. "No, sir. The worm is advancing, and we've been unable to do anything other than take some of the servers off the grid."

"How long is it going to take to restore control?"

The captain looked up at him. "Sir, I… our early reports are showing that as the worm works through the systems, it essentially eats up the structure. It may as well be formatting as it goes."

Thatle frowned, sternly. "What does that mean?"

The captain cleared his throat before answering. "It means," he said, his voice becoming unstable, "that if we're correct, our early diagnosis is showing that there will be nothing to restore in any of the systems where the attackers have been."

Thatle closed his eyes and paused before looking back at the captain. "Nothing?" he checked.

"Yes, sir. Nothing." The captain flinched a little, knowing what so often happens to the messenger.

The commander looked confused, hardly able to believe his ears. He didn't want to distract the captain from doing his job right now, but this required more problem-solving.

"Captain," he instructed, "can you assemble your best people for an investigative team, and send me the list in the next hour? Then bring in additional manpower to deal with the crisis. We're going to have to have a meeting with those who understand the problem, in order to come up with a solution."

The captain nodded, respectfully. "Yes, of course, sir. I'll get straight on it."

"Thank you, Captain," Thatle said quietly, before turning on his heels and heading back to his office.

*So much for being ready for the second attack*, he thought to himself grimly.

### On Board *The Empress*, Main cabin

"How are you getting on?" Oz asked Pieter through his implant.

Pieter flicked his wrist while he was typing, making sure his mic was open as he responded. "I'm trying to re-sequence the worm to take the comms out faster, but it's still going to be another ten minutes. I can't speed it up."

Oz tapped into what Pieter was working on.

"Yes, I see," he confirmed. "It was sequenced that way in the first place because it's the fastest way to take control of everything, given how their systems are structured."

Pieter stopped typing, and took a deep breath. "I've managed to speed up one loop by rearranging one of the small stacks of tasks; but, really, it's not making much difference."

He sighed in frustration. "Are the guys all right down there?"

"For the moment," Oz confirmed, his voice a little flat, even for an AI. "They haven't encountered any troops yet, but I think Molly can tell that they're closing in."

Pieter cocked his head and frowned. "What do you mean?" he asked.

"She's able to feel people around her," Oz explained. "Energetically."

Pieter was still frowning, and looking off above his open holoscreen. "This is a realm thing?" he asked.

"Yes," Oz confirmed. "Only thing is, it seems to weaken her the more people there are around, and the closer they get."

Pieter took a moment to realize the implications of what Oz was telling him. "This means she's going to have a problem when the troops catch up to them, then?" he asked.

Oz's voice was even more serious. "This is my concern. We've also lost eyes on the troops, and their communications have gone quiet. Was that you?"

Pieter checked something on his screen. "No - not yet."

"Okay," Oz continued. "They've probably moved their tactical onto quantum communicators. Now there's no way we can monitor them."

Pieter covered his mouth as he thought it through. "What can we do?" he mumbled back to Oz.

"Right now, just keep that worm working," Oz instructed. "I'm going to do a full frequency scan to see if I can pick up anything that might be useful. When that worm gets to the communications system, let me know, and we'll release the nanodrones."

"Okay," Pieter agreed. "Just need another few minutes."

## Planet Kurilia, Southern Hemisphere

Joel checked his map once more. "I think if we just keep going straight, we're going to hit it in another five minutes."

Jack followed behind him. "Sounds about right; although, if their troops are closing in, we probably want to think about evasive maneuvers."

Joel stopped and turned back to her. "You're probably correct." He glanced around trying to see what their options were, and being met with nothing but trees. "I'm thinking their nearest base to here is going to be off in that direction."

Jack put her hand over her eyes to shield them from the sun that was breaking through the tree cover. "So, if the target is that way," she said pointing in the direction they had been moving, "then they're going to be heading straight to it, to intercept us there."

She shook her head. "You know, it might just be worth heading straight there, in that case…"

Joel grimaced, "I think it's risky, either way. The other option would be to approach it from the left of where we are now; but if they control the target by the time we get there, we're done for, anyway."

Jack started moving again. "Okay, as we were. Let's keep going."

Just then, there was a faint buzz in the distance. Jack stopped in her tracks. "Do you hear that?"

Joel listened, standing perfectly still. "Yeah, like a swarm or something." He hit his holo. "Oz, have we got incoming?"

Oz responded through both their implants. "Yeah, but it's friendly. The buzz is the nanodrones fixing to the other targets we need to take out."

Joel sighed, and smiled at Jack as they started walking again. "Good to know."

"Yes," Oz replied. "But we've lost all trace of the troops. They've switched over to quantum, we think, and our worm has taken all of their other systems offline. You're essentially flying blind now."

Joel smiled grimly. "Well, this is what we thought might happen. Thanks for the heads-up, Oz."

"Sure. I'll keep you posted as things progress. Molly and Sean have reached their first target, and are doing a detour to get to their second."

"Okay. Thanks, Oz. Joel Out."

The pair of space marines kept moving at a brisk and quiet pace toward their target.


## Planet Kurilia, Northern Hemisphere

Molly looked up, sensing movement in the sky above her. Sean glanced over at her. "What is it?" he asked.

"Something's coming," she told him.

Sean looked up too. "Nanobot phase has started. That's a good sign, at least."

Molly brought her attention back down to the ground as they walked. She stopped.

Sean stopped and looked back at her. "Are you...? What is it?" he asked.

She cocked her head, listening. "We may need to course-correct again. I think they're closing in right ahead of us."

Sean shook his head. "What makes you think that?"

Molly put her head down, and rested her hands on her knees, bending over. "I... I can feel them. As I'm getting closer to people, it's zapping my energy. But I sense them, too."

She tried to stand up straight, but toppled a little. Sean grabbed her. "Dammit, Molly. You shouldn't have come. You're not right."

Molly didn't have the energy to argue with him. Her skin had turned gray, and her lips matched. Sweat was dripping off her, even though the climate and activity didn't warrant it.

"We need to go that way," she told him, pointing off into the undergrowth, away from the track they'd been following.

Sean resigned himself to the change in direction. He sighed. "Okay. Come on, then," he said, leading her. "Are you okay to walk?"

Molly nodded. "Yep, let's just keep moving," she said weakly.

### Planet Kurilia, Southern Hemisphere

Oz's voice connected through Joel's and Jack's implants. "Joel? Jack? I've just found something."

They continued to trudge through the sandy undergrowth toward their target. Joel wiped at his forehead.

"What is it Oz?" he asked, checking that the quantum link on his wrist was active.

"I've managed to get an image off one of their official military satellites," Oz told them. "It shows a section of the surface where you are."

"And?" asked Joel.

Jack had moved on, seeing glimpses of the clearing and their target just up ahead. She reached into her pants pocket to find the first charge to set.

Oz continued explaining his findings. "It looks like the troops are already at your target. The last frame before the satellite moved into range was them surrounding the generator."

Joel looked up at Jack disappearing ahead of him, towards the clearing. "Jack!" he called out to her, in a hushed, urgent whisper.

"It's okay," she called back quietly. "I've got this. I won't be a second."

Joel couldn't believe her recklessness. "Jack. They know we're here. They've got the place surrounded!" he hissed. "Oz, did she hear you?"

"I can't tell," Oz admitted.

Jack was ten paces ahead of Joel, and she didn't acknowledge. He started jogging toward her.

"Jack! Abort!"

Jack stepped out into the clearing and headed straight up to the building that housed the generator. She could see the green glow of the forcefield protecting it. A moment later, she had jogged up to it, and was placing the first charge.

Joel stepped out into the clearing, his weapon switched on, deployed and ready to fire if anything moved.

"Jack", he hissed again, scanning the tree line for any signs of Zhyn activity.

Jack disappeared around the other side to place the next charge.

"Damn it. Oz, she's already placing the charges!" Joel relayed.

"That means you're already at risk," Oz advised. "Get out of there. Get back to the skylift as quickly as you can."

Joel kept his eyes scanning all around him. All was quiet. He dug into his pocket, and moved the other way around the generator, preparing to set the other charges.

"Roger that, Oz," he agreed dryly. "If you've got a plan B, we might need some extra help."

Joel continued setting the charges around his side of the target.

# CHAPTER EIGHTEEN

**On Board *The Empress*, Main cabin**

Pieter looked up from his holo screen, and across at Maya and Paige. "You guys ready?" he asked them.

Maya nodded. "Yep. Whenever you are," she responded.

Paige started opening an array of holoscreens. Maya glanced over at her. "Let's do this," she grinned.

Paige nodded, anxious and excited.

Maya opened her screen, and started making the connections with the various broadcasting channels. "We've got all twenty-three of the major ones online."

Pieter called over the aisle to her. "Okay, just check that you can broadcast on each of them first, before you push out the first message."

Maya was quiet for a moment while she went through her checks. Paige finished what she was doing, and then looked over Maya's shoulder, watching her check each channel in turn.

"Okay, we're good," confirmed Maya.

Pieter set another program going. "Okay, start broadcasting now, and then set them on loop. If you can, let it all download onto their servers while its playing – it will continue to play long after we've left orbit."

Maya was working away, her tongue now sticking out from between her teeth on one side.

"K," she responded almost absently.

A few minutes later, she seemed to become aware of herself, and put her tongue back in her mouth. "Okay, Paige. If you can set the loop on each one as we go, I'll get them started?"

The cabin of the ship was quiet as the three of them worked away from their holoconnections to change the direction of the civilization on the planet beneath them.

### Planet Kurilia, Downtown Tarvok

"Hey, Rook, turn the sound up a moment, would you?"

The bartender turned to face his customer, and reached over to the controls.

"Of course," he smiled agreeably before turning back to the stack of glasses he was drying with a soft cloth.

The bar was quiet, it being the middle of a cycle, and apart from the couple sitting in a booth over on the far side, Rex was the only customer. He sat at the bar, his legs coiled around the stool he sat on, mostly keeping to himself and his beer.

"Ladies and Gentlefolk of Planet Kurilia," the broadcast on the hologram said. "It is with deep regret that we must inform you of some clandestine activities that have been happening on your planet."

"Hey, Rook, did you see this? Is this the news?" Rex called across again. His eyes betrayed his confusion at the strange broadcast.

Rook turned back and wandered over to where Rex was sitting and watching the holographic communication. "No. I've not. What channel is this?"

Rex shrugged. Rook picked up the controls and looked,

flicking through the preview of three other channels. "It's on every channel," he concluded, looking back at the screen.

The broadcast continued, with no visual other than a simulated changing pattern with a voiceover.

"As you know, you have a proud militia; a militia that is set to protect the Zhyn Empire, and its people. However, there has been operating an interplanetary clandestine force that seeks to break all treaties with the Federation – particularly the Jah-Dune Accord, which limits the size of each members' arms in the interest of peace."

Rex glanced at Rook. "Well, I'll be."

---

Less than ten miles north, in the Empire's government chambers, the same broadcast was heard by the Senate officials. An assistant got up from her desk and walked into her boss's office.

"Sir, there's something being broadcast that you ought to see."

Senator Aok looked up from his work and nodded. His assistant walked over to the control panel and put the hologram on for him, then stayed and listened, mesmerized.

"This force has been found to be secretly operating from the resources of your planet, encouraged by factions within your own government. To this end, these bases are being shut down. If this weren't done, then the planet would be at risk for violation of the Accord, essentially putting the citizens of the Empire at risk."

Aok didn't need to hear any more. "Get me a quantum link with the Lord High Marshall Shaa. This is going to cause a problem with the Federation."

The broadcast continued in the background, as Aok's office became a flurry of activity.

"These corrective measures have been taken, and this message is being communicated so that you are aware of what your government is doing – so that you can take a stand. If you take a stand, you will render these war-hungry factions null and void. If you allow them to move their operations into your civilian networks, though, you will face severe consequences; not just to your quality of life, but also to your planet's safety. We hope you choose to remain free, and hold your government accountable. A concerned third party."

The broadcast clicked off, and then restarted from the beginning of the message. "Ladies and Gentlefolk of Planet Kurilia. It is with deep regret that-"

By it's third playing, Aok was on the line with the Lord High Marshall Shaa's second in command, Davon.

"This clandestine operation is no longer so secretive," Aok told Davon. "I fully expect that the Emperor will be in touch shortly. I'll be issuing my full report to absolve myself from this debacle, though," Aok concluded.

Before Davon could respond, Aok had closed the connection and turned back to his console to continue working on his statement to absolve himself from any responsibilities.


**Planet Kurilia, Southern Hemisphere**

Jack placed the last charge. "Okay," she called to Joel, hearing footsteps shuffling in the undergrowth. She straightened up and headed around the last corner, expecting to see Joel placing the final charge.

Instead, she stepped around the corner and came face-to-face with an Estarian-looking Zhyn, who was a good three feet taller than her, with a weapon trained directly at her.

Instinctively, she backed away; her heart was in her mouth, but her training kicked in, despite the shock. Without looking around, she expanded her awareness to check where else a threat might be coming from. She tried to reach down to her holo to see if she could get in touch with Joel, but the Zhyn in front of her lunged forward and put the point of his blaster in front of her holo. He signaled for her to raise her hands in the air.

Jack complied, her mind racing and trying to figure out where Joel was, and if he'd been captured, too. Her eyes darted around, and she became aware of another two, three,six Zhyn emerging from the undergrowth and tree line. She backed up another couple of steps, and then felt another presence behind her. Spinning around, she came face-to-face with another Zhyn, who took the blaster off her shoulder – effectively leaving her defenseless.

"I'm here trying to save your people," she tried to explain. The Zhyn made some strange sounds back at her. *Language, dammit,* she thought to herself.

"Your secret military bases are in contravention to the Accord your government signed. I'm not here to hurt anyone, just to disable - "

The Zhyns continued talking and grunting between each other. The original creature began talking in her direction.

"I'm sorry. I don't understand what you're telling me…" she tried to explain, keeping her hands open and palms facing him, showing she wasn't a threat.

*Shit,* she thought to herself. She was scared, but she didn't get the sense that they were going to kill her right away.

If that was their intent, she'd be dead already.


**Planet Kurilia, Northern Hemisphere**

Molly stumbled and caught herself. She leaned her arm against the nearest tree, breathing hard.

Sean went on a few more paces before he realized she wasn't following. He turned and started walking back, anxiety in his eyes. "What's going on?" he asked her.

Molly tried to catch her breath, still looking gray and exhausted. "I think it's the number of people who are getting close."

Sean looked around, searching for some indication of how close the Zhyn really were. There was no sign of them yet… which meant they might have options. "We need to get back to the skylift," he announced decisively. "There's no way we can get to the second target, and then back – especially with you in this condition."

Molly couldn't argue. She leaned back against the tree and nodded.

*Oz. We need a route out.*

**Working on something. Can you maintain your location?**

*How long for?*

**A minute or two?**

*Maybe. I can feel them closing in.*

**Can you tell which direction?**

*Yes, from behind us.*

**So, then, keep moving. I've got a lock on you. I'm working on getting help to you.**

Molly was confused by his comment, but there wasn't time to clarify. She looked at Sean. "You're right. And I'm sorry. I agree, regarding the lifts; but the Zhyn are right behind us. We need to keep moving. Oz is working on getting some help to us."

Sean didn't look happy at all, but he nodded and grunted, and then helped Molly up off the tree. "Okay," he agreed, "Let me help you move faster."

He wrapped his arm under her arm and around her back, and helped her onward. Though it wasn't comfortable, what with Sean being about twice her width and a good few feet taller than her, she was glad of the help. The two moved through the wooded area a little faster, blasters still at the ready in case they were found.

**Planet Kurilia, Southern Hemisphere**

Jack tried to steady her breathing and maintain her alertness, as the discussions in the strange language continued around her. She still had her arms in the air, and it looked like there were still more Zhyn around in the area – even as new ones arrived, and a few others moved off deliberately in another direction.

Just then, the chatter seemed to increase in urgency and tone. Jack couldn't be sure, but there was a faint sound of a laser blast.

Then another.

She definitely heard that one.

There were sounds of return fire, the shrill ring of weapons she didn't recognize. Her captors surrounded her, putting their backs to her, and turning to face the new threat.

The one in front of her went down.

Then, one to her side. Two others started moving forward, searching the area for where the blasts were coming from. In seconds, each of them went down, and all was quiet again.

Jack moved forward, cautiously looking around for both Zhyns, and whoever had taken them out. She noticed the guy who had taken her own blaster, and picked it up from under his lifeless body, wriggling to get it free from under his hefty weight.

Her breathing was shallow as she kept her eyes peeled for any signs of life... Then she heard something to her left, just around the next corner of the generator building.

She ventured toward it, cautiously, treading as softly as she possibly could. Two steps later, a figure emerged, catching her off-balance.

She jumped, her heart pounding, and her finger ready to hit the trigger as soon as she was able to aim. And then she stopped, her mouth half-open.

"And next time, you won't run off on your own, yes?" Joel grinned back at her.

Jack exhaled sharply, trying to calm herself, not knowing whether she should laugh or cry.

"Son of a bitch!" she hissed at him, restraining herself from whacking him with the flat side of the blaster.

Joel hit the switch on his Zhyn-blaster, and it folded up into its more compact form. "That's no way to address the teammate who just saved your ass, young lady."

He kept walking, trying to get his bearings on their escape route.

Jack caught her breath and pulled up her holo.

"True. But you scared the living shit out of me. Hang on; I'm just contacting Oz, and then we need to get clear of this structure."

Joel nodded. "Agreed. Let's start moving this way. I'm willing to bet that when they don't hear back from their friends, they're going to send reinforcements along the same trail these guys came in on."

Jack followed after him as the quantum call connected.

"Oz. We've set the charges, and our target is ready to detonate when you are. We'll be clear in three minutes."

"Good," Oz replied through her implant. "Everything okay?"

"Yes, it is now. Joel ended up taking out a bunch of Zhyns, and we're expecting more to come after us. We're heading for the skylift now, but it will need to be an indirect route."

"Acknowledged," Oz confirmed. "I'm working on an extraction plan for you. Keep going. I have a location tracker on your quantum communicator so I know where you are, but we're still blind as to where the Zhyn are. Be careful."

"Understood, Jack whispered back. "Thanks, Oz."

Joel glanced back as Jack jogged to catch him up. "Okay," she said, "we need to move."

The two jogged out at double-time, keeping their wits about them as they moved.

CHAPTER NINETEEN

**Planet Kurilia, Capital Building of the Zhyn Empire**

Justicar Beno'or bustled through the great halls of the
Empire's capital building. His robes billowed as they caught the
air, making moving patterns of color in his wake. Heads turned
as eyes caught the normally-subdued and dignified Justicar
making his way to the Emperor's chamber at the center of the
complex of majestic halls and passageways.

Beno'or was undistracted by the attention. There was something far more important going on; a matter the Emperor needed
to be informed about. And Beno'or needed to be the one to tell
him – if another frame was introduced into the thinking, who
knew what war they might find themselves inciting?

He panted, willing his out-of-shape legs to carry him faster.

Finally he approached the main doors. There were two guards
in front of him. Normally, he would explain he had an appointment, but this time he couldn't say that. His cause was far more
urgent. He reached for the door handle himself, and a guard
moved to stop him. Beno'or looked up at the Zhyn, laden in ceremonial armor. "I need to speak to him. The fate of the Empire
rests on him knowing the information I have."

The guard hesitated a moment, clearly understanding who the Justicar was. He glanced briefly at his comrade on the other side of the doorway, then back at the Justicar, before relenting, and opening the door.

The Justicar nodded in gratitude, mumbling something about honor and the Empire as he shuffled through the half-open door.

Once inside, he took a moment to acclimatize and look around. The red plush carpets acoustically dampened the room; it was immediately quieter than the grandiose hall just outside the door. The lofty ceilings here were ornately painted, and pointed to the grandeur of the Empire's feelings about their Emperor.

Their ruler.

Their sole guardian and leader.

The Justicar bowed deeply, out of respect for the place and the status of the office, and then trod carefully. There was a corridor down to the right that ran alongside the main chamber; just up ahead was a door to the chamber where the Emperor received guests. Off to the left was a desk where the High Majesty's assistant would organize who got to see him, and who had to wait outside.

There was no one there, though.

Beno'or stepped forward, carefully making his way just inside the door. He didn't want to cause offense by barging inside, and yet, what he had to share was all too important to stand on ceremony.

He cleared his throat. "Forgive me," he started. His voice echoed through the large, empty hall. The red carpeting behind him ended, leaving polished wooden flooring in front of him.

Nothing stirred.

Beno'or took a few more paces inside, searching the hall for any sign of the Emperor. "I'm sorry to intrude, Your Highness…"

Still no response.

He heard movement behind him, and spun round to see the

assistant returning. He stepped back out to the red carpet area, and met with acute disapproval.

"Forgive the intrusion," Beno'or started. "I have an urgent matter to discuss with His Highness. The Empire hangs in the balance."

The assistant's expression changed from one of scorn to one of anxiety, and a willingness to help. "Let me tell him you're here," she said quietly as she disappeared down the corridor along the side of the chamber.

Beno'or waited for what seemed an eternity; but in actuality, was probably only a few minutes, augmented by his anxiety.

The assistant came back, striding purposefully as she announced, "Please, His Highness will see you now."

Beno'or entered the chamber again and made his way down to the front of the room to find the Emperor on his throne, on the elevated platform. There were the usual ceremonial tables in front of him, with chairs for the longer conferences.

"Your Highness," Beno'or said, bowing to his Emperor. "I have news of utmost importance."

The Emperor waved his hand. "Please, speak Beno'or. You have my attention." The Emperor's expression was one of concern.

Beno'or straightened up. "I'll come straight to the point, Your Highness. It seems that our own military has been arming themselves with secret bases, and weapons beyond what we knew."

The Emperor's air of concern turned to one of horror, but he remained silent, wanting to hear more.

Beno'or continued. "It seems some other faction from outside the Zhyn Empire has come to know about this, and found it to be in breach of the Jah-Dune Accord. As such, less than an hour ago, our defenses were breached, and the clandestine bases are being systematically destroyed in both a nanobot and cyber attack."

The Empereror looked about to speak, but Beno'or interrupted. "Forgive me, My Lord, but there is something else." He paused, not quite knowing how to relay the next piece of news. "It seems they have revealed the existence of these bases to our public. They have been broadcasting a message on all channels, on a loop, for the last ten minutes."

The Emperor closed his mouth, processing the information. He was silent for several moments before he spoke again. "Beno'or, tell me... As one of my most trusted advisors, did you know about the other bases?"

Beno'or answered immediately. "No, My Lord." His eyes were as shocked and concerned as the Emperor's.

"Then it seems," the Emperor continued, "that we have a case of treason on our hands. Do we know who was in charge of this clandestine operation?"

Beno'or looked down at his hands, and wrung his fingers together. "I have only my suspicions, Your Highness. Without proof..." he didn't finish his sentence.

The Emperor nodded sympathetically. "I understand. You're an honorable man, Beno'or. But events have forced us to be less careful with our words. If you have suspicions, I implore you to tell me."

Beno'or's head was still lowered in shame and regret as he uttered the words he knew The Emperor already suspected.

"I believe it was the Lord High Marshall behind this, Your Majesty."

### Planet Kurilia, Southern Hemisphere

"Okay, Oz," Joel said over the quantum link. "We're approaching the skylift now. How's Molly doing?" he asked.

Oz responded immediately. "Molly and Sean are on their way back to their skylift, too. They have Zhyns in pursuit."

"Shit," Joel cussed under his breath, still focused on moving as fast as he could. "Anything you can do to help them?"

"Yes," Oz confirmed calmly. "I'm working on it."

Joel glanced over at Jack as they jogged up to the lift. Jack hit the button, then doubled-over, catching her breath while they waited.

Joel put his free hand on his hip, the other holding his blaster. His eyes scanned the area, watching for any disturbance in the foliage.

Jack turned and looked at the lift panel again. She hit the button... again.

Joel smiled at her. "You know they're programmed to take twice as long each time you hit them, right?"

Jack looked at him, shocked. "Really?" she asked.

Joel's smile broadened. "No. I'm just messing with you."

She chuckled, and smacked him playfully, almost recovering her breath.

"Oz," Joel spoke again, hitting his quantum bead. "Anything you can do to speed up this skylift?" he asked.

Oz spoke into both their audio implants. "Hang on," he replied.

The pair waited, recovering their breath and their wits, while scanning their surroundings.

Oz's voice returned to the line. "Oh, heck. Problem."

Jack saw Joel's face drop. "What is it?" she asked, turning to check the panel for the lift. She looked, and then pressed at it again. "It's dead," she told Joel.

"Did you get that, Oz?" Joel checked.

"Yes. I just realized, too. They took them offline before we took control. We're locked out."

Joel shook his head, scrambling in his mind for other options, while watching for the slightest sign of trouble.

"Okay, Oz, we need a plan B, then."

Oz paused, as if he was multitasking, before responding. "Okay, coming right up. In the meantime, be careful to avoid those Zhyns."

Oz's audio went dead.

. . .

**Planet Kurilia, Capital Building of the Zhyn Empire**

The Lord High Marshall Shaa was sitting at his console, wading through the reports he was receiving in response to the attack on his bases.

The message from the intruders played on a loop in the background as he tried to fathom who might have done this. The Federation was the obvious choice, and yet they claimed no responsibility. Heck, how were they even to know that he was arming up as he was? Their communications were encrypted, and in a new language that the Federation had no access to. He'd taken every precaution.

That left either a rogue faction within the Federation who had somehow managed to access their most classified material, or someone who had a vested interest in seeing them controlled by the Federation.

He wracked his brains trying to think.

*It could be anyone...* he sighed. *Though the team who breached us was definitely human.*

He flicked through to the next cyber report on his console. More bad news. He held his head in his hand as his eyes reluctantly scanned the intel. With each piece of news, his stomach sank a bit more; bringing him closer and closer to internal despair.

His console beeped, and a light flashed, indicating a call. He accepted the communication, and the hologram opened up in front of his desk. It was Davon.

"Your Highness," Davon greeted him.

"Davon. You have news?" Shaa asked.

"Yes, Your Highness." Davon's voice was brighter than earlier that day. "Good news. We're about to apprehend both sets of intruders – our troops are closing in on them. The lifts have been deactivated, and they have no means of escape."

The Lord High Marshall relaxed back into his console chair. "Good," he responded. "This is indeed good news." He paused, contemplating the myriad of problems they still had yet to solve. "And what of the media channels? Can we shut those down?" he asked.

Davon nodded. "We're working on it, Your Highness, but we're encountering resistance at the broadcast stations."

Shaa's big brow creased across his forehead, making him look angrier than he actually was. "How so?" he pressed.

Davon glanced down at the floor before responding. "They're suggesting that if there is any element of truth in these things, the people have the right to know."

Shaa answered immediately. "Well, we have means of persuasion," he stated flatly, somewhat confused as to why this wasn't already in hand.

Davon nodded vigorously. "Yes, indeed, sir. And some have yielded already. It's just a matter of time," he said, before realizing his master needed more than that. "I'll take care of it," he added.

Shaa looked somewhat appeased. "Good. Thank you, Davon," he said, reaching over to the console panel to end the call.

"There's one more thing, Your Highness," Davon added.

Shaa's finger came back from the button, and he leaned back in his chair again.

Davon continued. "You should know," he explained quickly, "Beno'or was seen going to meet with The Emperor."

There was a long silence on the line.

Davon shifted awkwardly on the other end of the call, waiting for a reaction.

"Do we know anything else?" Shaa asked slowly, his face giving nothing away.

Davon was wringing his fingers again. "Not yet, my Lord."

Shaa took a deep breath, before responding. "Okay, thank you Davon," he said, and reached forward to end the call again.

The line disconnected, and Shaa sat back, turning his chair to look out of the large windows.

He could run.

He could always run.

But then he would be marked a criminal. He would be a terrorist rather than a hero.

*No.*

He needed to stay and make his case – whatever the implications of that were.

He stood up and straightened his uniform, then wandered over to his personal cabinet on the far side of the enormous room. He opened the door and pulled out a bottle with a green herby liquid in it. He found an antigrav tumbler, and poured himself a drink.

Then, taking both the bottle and the tumbler back to his console, he sat back down to await his destiny.


## Planet Kurilia, Northern Hemisphere

"They're catching up to us, Sean," Molly panted. Sean kept trying to keep her moving, but she was struggling.

"I can feel them," she insisted. "They're practically on top of us."

Sean looked around, trying to figure out another plan.

He helped Molly lean against another tree, and assisted her in opening up her blaster. "You good to point and shoot?" he asked her, his eyes revealing the emotional strain he was under.

She nodded, exhausted.

Sean gritted his teeth and picked up his own blaster, opening it into its ready position.

Molly held her blaster as best she could. "Are you set to stun or kill?" she asked.

Sean didn't answer. Instead, he just scanned the woodland in front of them.

"The minute you see anything move, start shooting," he told her.

*Oz. If you have any words of advice, now would be the time.*

**I have a few,** he responded. **How about, 'climb on board fast'?**

Molly frowned, confused.

Just then, she saw a blue face appear in the foliage in front of them. She hesitated, and suddenly there were another two.

Sean opened fire, and both went down, lights and lasers flying from his weapon in fast succession.

Then there was movement above them.

Molly looked up to catch sight of a pod dropping down to the surface. She felt a flood of relief, and a pang of familiarity at the sight of the rescue vehicle.

*Oz, you're a fucking genius!*

**I know. Now get on board.**

Molly glanced over to see Sean in full Rambo mode.

"Sean!" she called out. She pointed up at the pod, which quickly came to rest between them and their attackers. The pod door slid open, and Molly started moving toward it.

Sean kept laying down cover, allowing her the opportunity to climb in. As soon as she was aboard, he ran over to join her. With one last blast of his weapon, he jumped in after her, and hit the button for the door to close.

*Okay, we're in*, Molly told Oz.

Emma's voice came over the pod. "Oz is busy at the moment, so I thought I'd step in and help."

Sean exhaled and laughed, tapping on the wall of the pod affectionately. "Nice to hear you, Emma. Thanks for the rescue."

"Anytime, Sean Royale," she replied. "I'd miss you if you weren't around."

Sean nodded.

Molly smirked, despite her condition. "Didn't think you were the kind of guy to develop friendships," she teased, quietly noticing how the guy could charm the pants of even an EI.

Sean pulled a face at her. "You'd be surprised, Molly Bates. Most people like me."

Molly visibly rolled her eyes at him, and sat back in the seat. She slumped over to one side, allowing the pod wall to support her; her relief was written all over her face.

Sean wasn't happy with her condition.

"Tell you what," he said to her. "How about when we get you back to *The Empress*, you let Emma check you out in the med bay?"

Molly nodded sleepily, closing her eyes. "Sure. As long as I don't have to walk anywhere," she whispered, before drifting off.

Sean checked her pulse and made sure she was breathing okay, then let her relax.

### Planet Kurilia, Southern Hemisphere

Joel and Jack stood poised, scanning the area for Zhyns, when Oz's voice came over their implants.

"Emma says if you can maintain your location, she'll have some help to you in less than ten seconds," he told them.

Joel checked his holo link. "Any help would be greatly appreciated at this point, Oz."

He searched the sky, or at least what they could see of it beyond the trees. Jack glanced over at him. "They're sending pods?"

Joel nodded. "I think so."

Jack shifted her blaster on her arm, trying to get more comfortable. She put her other hand on her hip, resting. All the time she kept scanning their surroundings, just in case.

Hardly five seconds later, a pod descended straight down to stop just above the ground in front of them. The door slid open, and Joel and Jack ran forward and clambered in.

The pod took off again, even before the door was fully closed.

"Wow, that was a close call," Joel commented, looking out of the window and seeing the forest ahead of them teaming with Zhyns ready to take them down.

Jack glanced down briefly, then sat back, exhaling. "I'll say. I'm ready for a vacation."

Joel grinned. "Sounds like a plan. Where are you thinking? Somewhere with a beach?"

Jack smiled, collapsing her blaster down and pushing it under the seat. "I was thinking somewhere more rocky, with artificial gravity."

Joel chuckled.

Emma piped in. "I know just the place for you!" she exclaimed brightly.

All three of them laughed as the pod whisked them away, out of the Kurilian atmosphere.

## On Board *The Empress*, Main cabin

Emotions were running high in the cabin-cum-hacker-room.

Maya and Paige were celebrating as they watched the counters clock the number of times their broadcast had run on each channel. The algorithm that estimated how many millions of people had seen their broadcast also kept climbing; though its increase was slowing down now.

"That's nearly 2.4 billion!" Paige exclaimed.

Maya grinned. "Yep. Not bad for one broadcast."

Paige glanced over at her. "Have you ever had one of your broadcasts reach so many people before?"

Maya shook her head. "Nope, this is my first time in the billion range." She shrugged casually, like it was nothing, but Paige could see she was quietly pleased at the reach of their work.

Their excitement was tempered only by the sheer concentration that Pieter was going through. The worm had hit a few sticking points, and he and Oz were doing everything they could to make sure they were able to do everything they still needed to.

"Just one more piece, and we're through," Pieter said to Oz.

Oz's voice came through over the cabin audio. "Agreed. The nanobots are all in place, and all but one of the generator targets are ready to blow."

Pieter frowned, distracted. He finished typing. "What did you say about all but one of the targets?"

Oz switched to Pieter's implant to communicate. "Molly and Sean needed extracting before they were able to lay the charges," he explained.

Pieter shook his head. "That sucks. We'll have to just go without it, then."

Oz agreed. "Yes. But in good news…" Pieter's screens were a flurry of activity, even drawing Maya's eye from across the aisle. She watched the screens pile up.

"What happened?" she asked.

Pieter sat back and grinned. "We're through," he told her. "The worm is all the way through every system, and is doing its thing as we speak."

Paige clapped her hands. "Yay!"

She and Maya high-fived, and then Pieter put his hand across the aisle to high-five them, too.

"Good going!" Maya congratulated him, slapping his raised hand gently before leaning out of the way so he could reach Paige.

"Yeah, great teamwork," he grinned. "And," he peered over at her screens, "looks like your campaign is doing well, too."

She nodded. "Yup. Just like magic," she agreed.

"Okay, Oz," Pieter confirmed, "as soon as the boss's team gets back, I think you're all set for the final phase."

Oz spoke through the cabin audio again. "I do believe we are," he agreed.

The tension had finally lifted from the cabin, and was replaced by an air of celebration.

## Planet Kurilia, Leaving the Northern Hemisphere

Molly opened her eyes a little, and stretched out.

"You still with us?" Sean asked, glancing down at her as they rode in the pod up into the atmosphere.

"Yeah. I'm still here," she told him as she sat up. "Actually, I'm feeling a bit better." Her face seemed to be getting some life back into it.

Sean cleared his throat. "Look, er," he hesitated a moment. "I'm sorry I came down so hard on you down there - about you not being fit for the mission."

Molly shrugged, holding onto the handrail and leaning to look down at the planet they were leaving behind.

"It's okay. You were right," she admitted.

Sean tilted his head from side to side. "Yeah, but I was also a dick."

Molly pushed her bottom lip out, in indifference. "I'm used to that bit," she said, not able to stop her lips from breaking into a smile.

Sean grinned back at her. "Well, great. So I'm gonna assume that's apology accepted, then."

Molly continued to look out of the window in front of them. "Sure," she said simply.

Sean knew what that meant, but he had no idea what else to do about it. Then something else occurred to him.

"Hey, Emma, what's going to happen about our second target?"

Emma's audio channel opened up again. "I believe that Oz intends to proceed as planned, just without that target being blown up."

Molly frowned, calculating the effects that would have on

their overall plan. She shook her head. "How about we go get our second target?" she proposed.

"That's the best suggestion you've had all day," he agreed, looking more lively.

*Oz, we're going to lay the charges for the second target. Wanna hold off blowing the fuck out of everything until then?*

**Sure, we've just got the worm complete, so we're ready to blow the charges and the nanodrones as soon as you're clear.**

*Okay, stand by. I'll let you know when we're out of the blast radius.*

Sean reached into his pocket and pulled out three charges. "Emma?" he said.

Emma responded. "Yes, Sean?"

Sean started doing up his combat jacket again. "Be a love, and take us down to our second target?"

Emma's voice lilted through the audio system, as if she too were keen to get back into the fight. "Of course," she answered, "rerouting now."

The pod veered off at an angle back down towards the surface, taking the pair to complete the mission they had originally set out to do.

# CHAPTER TWENTY

**On Board** *The Empress,* **Main Cabin**

Pieter scratched at his forehead. He was tired, but trying to understand the last piece of what they had already executed.

"So, even though the worm has destroyed all the firmware, you're saying that it can still report back anything that they try to reactivate?"

Oz spoke over the cabin audio. "That's exactly what I'm saying," he confirmed. "Plus, with the communications broadcasts, I uploaded a patch onto their civilian systems that will enable us to keep an eye on things, too."

Pieter smiled broadly. "Bloody hell, Oz. You're a frikkin' genius!"

Oz chuckled, his laughter filling the cabin. "Yeah. I think I get it from Molly."

Paige and Maya heard the tail-end of the conversation, and started chuckling away.

"But," Oz added, "I couldn't have done it without you, Pieter."

Pieter blushed a little. "Aww, Oz," he said, carefully avoiding eye contact with the girls, "that's the sweetest thing you've ever said to me."

Oz chuckled. "Well, don't get all mushy on me, bro. I just appreciate you."

Pieter leaned forward and hugged his holo.

Paige giggled. "Oz, he's hugging his holo, in order to give you a hug."

Oz's voice sounded a little different. Even emotional.

"If I had a face, I'd be blushing," he remarked.

There were chuckles and more banter between the team members.

"Hang on," Oz said suddenly.

The laughter died down.

"Okay," Oz reported. "Molly just said they're clear. Let's blow these nanobots and quantum charges, Pieter!"

"It would be an honor," Pieter agreed, as he turned his attention back to his holo and hit a few keys.

He looked over at Paige and Maya. "You may be able to see some of the explosions on the surface from one of the windows," he said, nodding over to the far side of the cabin. The two girls scrambled up and headed over to see. Pieter followed them, carefully closing up his holo as he moved.

"Wow," Paige gasped as she reached the window. "It's so pretty!"

Maya nodded silently.

The orange explosions could be seen from their altitude, and the faint ripple of the forcefield was a hint of green that quickly disappeared.

**On Board *The Empress*, Downstairs hangar deck**

Molly and Sean's pod arrived back into the pod bay of *The Empress*, and the tailgate closed behind them. Joel and Jack had already returned, and were undoing their body armor and removing their holsters. They were exhausted, but somewhat pumped from their ordeal.

The incoming pod touched down, and the door slid open. "Thanks, Emma," Sean said, as he stepped out. He turned around, and offered a hand to Molly.

Brock watched her actually take it.

"Girl, are you okay?" he asked, walking over to the pod to also help her out. "You're pale as anything." He glanced at Sean, and then at Sean's hand, which Molly still held. Sean noticed, and looked at him as if to say, *"whaaaa?"*

Molly nodded. "I'll be fine," she said, smiling. Her hair was wet with sweat, and she could barely stand on her own.

Joel glanced at her, and then at the view outside of the closing tailgate.

"Check out your handy work down there. That's the northern hemisphere targets," he remarked.

Molly walked around to the other side of the pod to catch the last glimpse of the view before the doors closed.

"Ours," she said, glancing at Sean. "All of our handy work," she added, smiling at Jack and Joel, too.

Joel bobbed his head, fiddling with an arm guard he'd just removed. "Mission complete, then," he announced.

"Right lady," Sean said turning back to Molly, "You promised you'd let me take you to the med bay, to let Emma check you out."

Molly nodded weakly. "Okay. Let's go," she agreed.

Joel frowned, concerned.

Sean picked her up, and started carrying her in his arms. "Heyyyyyyy!" she protested.

Joel and Jack started laughing. Brock stood watching, shaking his head.

"Alphas," he muttered under his breath, raising his eyes to the ceiling.

Jack nudged his arm playfully and smiled. "Yeah," she agreed.

"Emma," Joel called so that she could hear him. "Wanna let Crash know we're all back, and ready to leave?"

"Sure thing, Joel. Telling him now," Emma confirmed.

. . .

## Planet Kurilia, Capital Building of the Zhyn Empire

The Emperor of the Zhyn Empire stepped from his private chambers into the main hall. His closest advisors were assembled, along with the man he had previously regarded as the protector of the Empire: The Lord High Marshall Shaa.

Shaa was in full military dress, surrounded by six of the Emperor's personal guard. Shaa wore a look of indignation; a hint of defiance quietly coloring the edges of his eyes.

The Emperor made his way to his throne, and nodded to his subjects. Those at the ceremonial desks took this as their cue to be seated, and pulled up their holographic devices from the consoles.

The Emperor began. "Lord High Marshall Shaa, you have been brought before me to answer on counts of treason. We know about your covert activities to over-arm our planet, and I would like to hear what you have to say for yourself."

Shaa was silent for a moment, but the Emperor had the presence to hold the space for an answer.

Finally Shaa responded.

"You think that by getting rid of me you will get rid of the problem? You have no idea how many in your service agree with my actions. We want the Zhyn Empire to be great again, and that is a desire that runs through our blood. We are many, and we are proud. We will not kneel before the Federation. You mark my words, Your Highness; this is not over. The Zhyn Empire will rise again."

The Emperor considered the position of the man before him. He held his gaze from his elevated position on his throne. The traitor's eyes remained dark and hostile. He was angry that he was misunderstood, and incensed by the notion that he had to go out on his own to acquire the power he wanted.

The consorts shifted awkwardly in their seats, curious as to how the Emperor might respond to such insults.

The guards remained motionless and emotionless, holding their prisoner between them – regardless of his politics, or the fact that he used to be their commander's commander, before he was escorted into this room.

The Emperor breathed deeply, and allowed the glare to be broken. He stood from his throne and walked forward on his platform, causing a stir amongst those who observed the interaction. "I will not risk the lives of the Empire for your political gain. You chose power over honor; you have disgraced your Empire and your position."

Shaa protested, his voice rising. "What I do, I do for the Zhyn Empire! You, My Lord, are making the Empire weak. You're making us into the Federation's pet! But we are a proud people – we will not be tamed. We will not be controlled. We will not yield to weak leadership."

Though Shaa's outburst elevated the tone of the conversation, the Emperor remained calm and unflustered.

"You will leave the Zhyn Empire, and live out your days in exile."

He returned to his throne and sat down. "So it is," he decreed.

The guards changed their formation, taking hold of Shaa so there was no means of escape, and led him back out of the chamber backwards, so he could not turn his back on The Emperor.

There were whispers and titters from the advisors and the consorts who sat watching the proceedings as witnesses to the interaction and exile.

Once the guards and prisoner were gone, the tall doors at the end of the room were closed, leaving the remaining company to resolve the issues they now faced.

The Emperor called upon his Justicar.

"Beno'or," he called.

Beno'or stood up from behind a console, and stepped out onto the main floor in front of the platform. He bowed.

"Yes, Your Highness?"

"Please set up a call with the Federation. This cannot go unanswered."

Beno'or bowed again, and backed away from the main floor space before turning and leaving the chamber.

Once his face was turned, he allowed his anxiety to show. The call he was about to set up could mean anything.

*Was the Emperor going to apologize? Or demand retribution? Was this going to be worse than what Shaa had planned?*

His stomach turned as the doors closed behind him, and he stepped out on the red carpet.

# CHAPTER TWENTY-ONE

**Gaitune-67, Safe house, Molly's Quarters**

"So what did Emma say?" Joel asked casually as he lounged across the bed.

Molly pulled her lips down, nonchalantly. "That there's nothing wrong with me," she said. "Physically."

Joel shifted up onto one elbow to rest his head on his hand. "So what's going on, then?"

Molly shook her head. "Seems I'm able to feel everything that's going on with people, and it just gets to be too much." She paused, and looked down. "I take it Sean told you what happened on the surface?"

Joel nodded grimly. "Yeah, he told me briefly; but he didn't have an explanation."

Molly sighed. "I don't know if *I* have an explanation. All I know is that I become awash with knowing other people's feelings when they get close, and that on the mission, with all those Zhyns after us, and us all amped up, it was just too much."

Joel sat up and perched on the edge of the bed, his back to her. "What are you going to do?" he asked.

Molly shrugged. "Another Vision Quest, I guess. I mean,

things have certainly moved on. I can control the realm-shifting now, so I don't see any reason why I wouldn't be able to control this."

Joel turned to face her, pulling his leg up on the bed in front of him now. "That sounds… positive."

Molly smiled. "Yeah. I think it is. I'm not as concerned about it as I was with the initial problems. There's a way forward."

She drifted off a little, and then brought herself back to the conversation.

"The thing that bothers me is having to feel all this shit, though. I… I don't like it. Heck," she smiled a little, "I don't even like feeling my own feelings, let alone anyone else's!"

Joel grinned. "Yeah, I can appreciate that," he agreed, support-ively. "But you know what I think?"

Molly shook her head, her brown hair bouncing around her face. "No… what?"

Joel looked seriously at her now. "I think it's what you asked for, in some way."

Molly frowned. "How d'you mean?"

Joel looked down at the blanket they were sitting on, and traced a pattern with his finger. "Well, your biggest struggle with leading this team is understanding things from their perspective. Being able to empathize and relate."

"Yeeeeees?" Molly agreed slowly.

"Well," Joel continued, "if you've suddenly got this ability to tune in and feel, or understand something, from someone else's perspective – I'd say that's a distinct advantage."

Molly's mouth dropped open as she froze, contemplating the sudden reframe.

"I… I suppose you're right," she said quietly after a few moments. "I mean, if I can control this so that I'm not over-whelmed by it all, then it could become a useful managerial tool." Her voice had switched into her normal, task-orientated, utili-tarian mode.

Joel chuckled to himself, closing his eyes and shaking his head gently.

"Whaaa?" Molly asked, suddenly aware that he was mocking her.

"Nothing." he said. "This is a possibility for you to expand your understanding of people for yourself, and you immediately equate that to how you can use it to solve a specific work problem. It's just…"

Molly cocked her head. "Sad?" she ventured.

"No," Joel told her. "Adorkable."

Molly smiled at his conflation of words to describe her. "Right. Thanks, Joel. Really… great…" she said, a hint of playful sarcasm hanging from her words.

There was a knock at the door.

"Come in!" called Joel.

Molly scowled at him. "Hey, it's *my* room!" she told him. "Come in!" she called, copying his tone and intonation, a glint in her eye.

The door swooshed open to reveal Paige, standing with a parcel in her hands.

"Hope I'm not interrupting," she said, raising her eyebrows up and down suggestively and regarding them both sitting on the bed.

Without waiting for an answer she strode in, her high heels heralding her arrival, and tossed the package casually across the room to land on the bed in front of Molly. "Shipment just came in from the Zon," she told her.

Joel looked curious. "What is it?" he asked, then immediately wishing he hadn't.

Paige winked. "Girly stuff," she grinned.

Joel blushed as he shook his head, making himself promise he would never walk straight into such a potential landmine again.

"Right. Er. Sorry," he said, standing up.

Molly watched, a small smile on her face, having no intention of alleviating Joel's embarrassment.

Joel hitched his belt a little and scratched the back of his head. Then he turned, and smiled at Molly. "I'll, er, see you in the kitchen in a bit, then…"

Molly frowned slightly.

Paige jumped in to remind her.

"Pizza! It's our post-operation pizza celebration!" she declared. "You know… our *tradition*."

"Ooohh," Molly sighed, realizing what time of day it was, and then putting it all together with the mission they had just completed. She shook her head briefly, trying to ground herself back in the reality everyone else operated in.

"Sure," she told Joel. "See you in there."

Joel waved and left, the door swooshing shut behind him. Paige waited for a second to make sure he was out of earshot, and then grinned excitedly.

"Okay, are we going to do this, or what?"

Molly looked down at the self-dyeing chemical kit. "Yeah, I guess so. I mean, in the absence of a genetics lab, it's our best option."

Paige shrugged. "I think so. Unless you want to ask the General if you can perform your genetic experiments through one of his precious pod docs…?"

"Errr, no," Molly said definitely. "High maintenance, dumbass chemicals it is," she said as she scrambled off the bed and headed to the bathroom.

Paige skipped after her, a glint in her eyes. "It's going to be *fabulous*!"

## Gaitune-67, Safe house, Kitchen

An hour later, the team was starting to congregate in the kitchen. Joel, Sean, Jack, and Crash were already sitting around drinking beer. Pieter, Brock, and Maya had gone out to pick up pizza. Molly and Paige's location was unknown.

Oz was hooked in over the intercom in the kitchen, explaining some of the finer points of the Many-Worlds Theory.

Joel scratched the top of his head with one hand, while placing his beer down with the other. "So what you're saying is that Molly effectively tuned in to one of the likely possible futures, and that's how she saw Crash on the floor before it happened?"

"Yes," Oz agreed, "although, the exact timeline is a little hazy. I was deactivated, and although Emma has a time log for when Crash left the ship, Molly doesn't have a running time code for the various events on her Vision Quest."

Joel frowned. "What about her memory?"

"Well," Oz considered his words carefully as he spoke, "she would have had to look at her holo; but then, you know what Molly is like with time."

Sean and Joel looked at each other, and put on their best Molly-accents. "Irrelevant," they said together, and then burst out laughing before clinking their beer bottles.

Jack sat upright, chuckling quietly at the boys, her chest bouncing up and down as she laughed. "You guys really pay a lot of attention to what Molly does, eh?" she observed before taking another swig of beer.

"No, no," Joel protested. "It's not that. It's just that she does so many things that are so damn funny…"

"…it's hard not to notice and remember them," Sean finished his sentence. The two looked at each other again, laughing. Jack shook her head, and couldn't help but join in.

She caught Crash's eye, and, even though Crash normally remained pretty stoic, even he seemed to be chuckling quietly at the interaction. He pulled his lips down at the corners and nodded his head, agreeing with Joel and Sean.

"Anyway," added Sean, "going back to this Many Worlds lark

– I wonder: is there some way we can harness this foresight to keep us out of trouble?"

Oz was still connected through the audio. "It's a good question. After all, *you*, Royale, need all the help you can get with that!"

Joel raised his bottle to Oz. "Nice one, Oz!"

The laughter spilled out into the foyer.

Oz stayed on-point, though. "I'll think about the implications though, Sean. What it would probably require is for Molly to do a few experiments to see if she can actually see forward in the timeline – which would be an interesting study in itself. I'm sure it will force us to reexamine our assumptions about reality."

"Well," Sean added, scratching his chin then taking another drink of his beer, "I'd be interested to know anything you find out."

At that moment, Pieter, Brock, and Maya walked into the kitchen with their atmosuits on, carrying stacks of pizza boxes and beer.

"Grub's up!" announced Maya, and the warriors stood up and started making themselves busy, setting the table and arranging the pizza boxes as they were dumped onto the table.

Pieter disappeared again to get rid of his gear, and, after grabbing a beer each and cheersing each other, Maya and Brock did the same.

Jack sat back down once they had everything ready to eat. "Someone should let Paige and Molly know that - "

Paige walked in.

"It's okay. We're here." She was grinning widely from ear to ear. As soon as Molly followed her into the kitchen, it was clear *why*.

"Oh, my," Jack exclaimed, her eyebrows raised taking in Molly's look. "You changed your hair back! It looks great."

Molly looked a little embarrassed. "Thank you," she said

before grabbing herself a beer from the fridge and handing it to Joel, who took the lid off for her.

Joel handed her beer back, topless. "So, that was the thing," he commented, referring to the package that Paige had shown up with at Molly's door.

Molly nodded, smiling. "Yeah, that was the thing."

He frowned a little. "But this wasn't another genetic experiment?"

Molly shook her head. "Nope. Not this time. This is boring old chemicals, which I'll have to keep applying every few weeks as the hair grows... No genetics lab here to do the thing that made it blonde in the first place."

Joel nodded. "I see. And you didn't want to stay natural?"

Molly shook her head again, her newly-bleached hair falling in her eyes, still a little damp from the shower.

"No. I wanted to feel like my old self again," she told him quietly.

Joel smiled, and then pointed his beer at her to chink. "Well, welcome back, Ms. Bates. Good to see you again."

Molly grinned and chinked her bottleneck against his. "Why, thank you, Mr. Dunham. It's good to *be* back."

While they were talking, the rest of the team had organized themselves around the table and started dishing out pizza. Molly and Joel joined them, and the normal hush fell over the group.

Eventually, as the eating slowed and the laughing and talking increased again, Maya nudged Paige.

"Now is as good a time as any," she told her, looking pointedly in Molly's direction.

Molly caught on that they were about to include her in the conversation. Paige looked suddenly shy. Her chest flushed deep red.

Maya insisted, though. "Go on. Tell her."

Paige swallowed, gathered her courage, and put the crust of her pizza down on her plate.

Molly kept chewing.

"Molly," Paige said across the table. "Maya thinks I should run this by you. It's about the nail varnish company."

Molly took another bite of meat-free pizza, her attention turned to Paige.

"Uh huh," she said through the cheese.

"Well," Paige continued, "things are progressing. The articles we've been writing have been causing a stir, and it looks like Oz has found the best manufacturing plant for the operation. We've got a great deal, and all being well, it looks like if we were to manufacture this first shipment, it could probably all be sold through this first Newstainment offer we're going to run."

Molly kept chewing, suspecting what was coming next.

Paige paused to draw breath, and then took a quick swig of her beer.

Maya was watching Molly intently, ready to gauge her reaction.

Paige spoke up again. "So if it all goes okay, we're looking at a 20% ROI for any investor that puts some money down for us to get the first shipment manufactured."

Molly smiled at her, knowing what Maya was up to and answered quickly. "Of course, Paige. I'd love to."

Paige grinned, relieved.

Maya was smiling too, but pretending to be offended at how easy Molly made it for Paige. "Hey!" she exclaimed. "You didn't even make her make you an offer. She didn't even have to ask for the business!"

Molly chuckled. "I know. I just didn't want her to have to suffer any more than you were already making her."

Maya smiled and pretended to huff.

"Well…" she said. "You try and help a girl out, and then everyone makes out like you're the bad one."

Paige put her beer down on the table, and turned and hugged Maya. "Thank you for helping me," she said.

The rest of the table had stopped and was watching what was playing out.

Maya patted Paige on the back as she hugged her back. "You're welcome. Just make sure you go and make a shit ton of money," she told her.

Paige nodded, and then got up. She walked around the table, fully aware that all eyes were now on her, but not caring. She shuffled around to where Molly was sitting and bent down and hugged her, too. "Thank you for believing in me," she told her, her eyes welling with tears.

When Paige released Molly and stepped back, she saw that Molly had tears in her eyes, too. "You're very welcome, Paige," Molly told her.

Paige shifted her feet awkwardly, unexpectedly self-conscious. She headed back around the table to sit down, and Molly searched for something to dry her eyes with.

Almost as if he were mind-reading, Joel produced a clean napkin from the pile in the center of the table, and handed it to her. She took it, smiling, the emotion welling up in her chest amplified by her newfound emotional awareness.

Joel put his hand on her back to comfort her, and Molly felt something she hadn't really been able to experience before. Something that surprised her.

She stopped crying, and tried to process it.

It was a feeling of real, *genuine* love and caring.

It threw her for a second, but when Joel removed his hand, it diminished but didn't go away. Everyone went back to their beer, pizzas, and conversations, and Joel was oblivious.

But Molly logged the new sets of data points to consider later.

Later, when she was less overwhelmed.

# EPILOGUE

*ArchAngel*

Giles bustled to leave the communications suite, pulling his tweed jacket on as he walked, and trying to connect a call.

He strode purposefully through the corridors of the *ArchAngel*, flustered, anxious, and excited, all at the same time.

The call went to messages.

"Hello, General," he started, managing to get one arm into the sleeve of his jacket. "I've, er, been talking with Arlene. We've put some pieces together; I really think we need to talk. Your concerns… You were right. Could you contact me at your earliest convenience, perhaps?"

He disconnected the call, and swung his arm into the other sleeve of his jacket, straightening it. Glancing down at his holo, he realized it was the middle of the night. But this couldn't wait.

He slowed, wondering what his next course of action should be. Having a new thought, he turned back the way he had come, and pulled up directions to the archive lab.

There was something critical he ought to check out before making any recommendations.

Hi Ascenders!

So I've just read MA's Author notes, and I have a few things to
~~correct~~ respond to.

**Dr. Genius.**

Ok, so MA has picked up on something that may or may not
have been there… How that conversation *actually* went was more
like:

Ellie, having told MA that she collapsed at the gym and was
feeling ill again, made some comment about how Dr. Genius had
suggested interval training.

MA: Oh so he's in the dog house now?

Ellie: I collapsed! Yes, he is.

(*Beat*)

Ok, in his defence, by interval training he probably meant
different heights on the treadmill. Not 30 minutes of running
and then 20 minutes of kick boxing.

Two days later…

MA: So how's Doctor Genius?

Ellie: I dunno. I haven't had another appointment.

MA: So he's still Dr. Genius, or has he been reverted back to Dr. Awesome?

>>> It seems MA has decided there is a sliding scale:

Dr Awesome – the guy, as he is normally.

Dr. Genius – his name when Ellie does something stupid like kick boxing too soon and suffers consequences.

Dr. Google - When *MA* looks up Ellie's symptoms and makes a diagnosis from Google.

*[ MA - WAIT A MINUTE, I don't think I'm the one was looking up the symptoms! You could barely get your head off a pillow, and I'm supposed to take the fall for your memory now, too?]*

*[ELLIE – I couldn't lift my head off of the pillow, YOU were the one Googling!]*

And he now has one more name that the Author's Editor came up with:

Jen: your Doctor sounds hilarious.

Ellie: Yeah. And he's CUTE.

Jen: BONUS. Hahaha, we should call him Dr. Hotsome...

Ellie of course realises that this is becoming so embarrassing she needs to just get the hell better so she doesn't need a doctor anymore.

---

Speaking of fun and amusement, one of the other things we (MA and I) have been up to is getting a submission in for South by South West (SXSW) – the conference for creatives.

Under my alter ego as a maverick entrepreneur I ran a Think Tank at the beginning of this year called: Storytelling for Social Profit. Basically it was a conference, with a Think Tank attached to it, where we posed the questions: how do we make the world a better place? And then how do we effectively weave this into a badass story?

Several weeks ago one of the Think Tank experts suggested we submit a panel to SXSW, based on this project.

Ellie: Yeah. Great idea. (Silently thinking what a baaaaaad idea it is given she can't even get up out of bed most days.)

Two weeks later... chin wagging with MA on one of our long rambling calls, Ellie explains the idea, and then finds herself suggesting MA makes up the fourth person. "Because look at all the awesome story shit you do, top 100 author... It will be a blast."

MA agrees.

3 days before the deadline...

Ellie: shit. Guess I should get something pulled together.

Emails her panellists to get bios, and inside leg measurements.

1 day before the deadline... with half of the Rebirth Manuscript still waiting to be punched up to be sent to Jen, having pulled our release date forward by 4 days (because MA is competitive! #justsayin')...

Ellie crawls out of bed at 8am (unheard of normally), puts on makeup, does hair, and records a sequence of narrative videos to insert between sample clips.

That was Friday.

Ellie worked on solidly the whole afternoon and evening, in order to turn around both the application/ video and Rebirth... on the same frikkin day.

Jen 'Editor-Extraordinaire' McDonnell then stayed up till nearly 2am to edit the rest of the MS so we could get it to the JITers for Saturday morning. Phew.

Regarding the SXSW application, I may, if MA agrees, share the link with you when it goes out to the public vote... My reason for this is four-fold:

1. We need the votes in order to get selected.

2. I'd like to share some of what we're working on in the background to help impact the world as writers.

3. We've got an awesome clip of MA doing his speaking

thing... and he manages to drop both and f-bomb (or more) AND says motherfucker, in like a 5 minute clip. He's HILARIOUS.

4. I regard the TKG community as my friends... and I know MA does too. Heck, at this point we're practically family. And I just want to share this other part of what we're doing with the family.

When that goes live, I'll ping you an update... either through the next author notes or on the fb page.

www.facebook.com/ellleighclarke

Ok, back to all things Kurtherian. Massive thanks must go to Jen for accomplishing such a short turn around, last into the night, and with a cheeriness.

I would also like to thank the incredible JIT team, and Zen-Steve their coordinator, for their incredible efforts so we don't embarrass ourselves with school girl errors.

I'd also like to thank my Icelandic friend, Trausti Traustason again for checking the Icelandic cussing and grammar. You da bomb, man. Thank you.

And of course, massive thanks must go to my long-suffering Yoda, without whom none of this would be possible. Dude, I know take the *micky* (look it up) something rotten, but you're the best. Thank you for the encouragement, the enthusiasm, the piss taking, and the constant stream of Slack messages. And I'm sorry your plan to get your fans asking for Molly book 5 backfired, and resulted in them asking you for BA book 18 in your reviews. That was them. I had nothing to do with it... and just laughed away in the corner when I saw what was happening. :)

Bwahahahahahahhahaha....

I'd also like to say a massive thank you to you, the readers, the fans and the reviewers. Your reviews and interaction with us are a CONSTANT source of encouragement and entertainment. Seriously, when there is a lull in a conversation what often happens is: "did you see so and so's review...". Or: "Lemme go check the 5* reviews." Or: "Dude, one of your fans messaged me to check your Darkest Night reviews and...."

You're the best. So *thank you*!

(P.S. I've been hearing you're making other authors jealous!)

### Michael and Competition

MA: Dammit Ellie.

Ellie: What?

MA: you're making me up my game with the formatting of my fucking author notes now!

Ellie: (blink blink)

### Michael and Admin Rights

I just wanted to close the loop on this one. You may have seen on fb some discussions about how MA has full admin rights to post on my page, and I have practically no admin rights to post on his.

It has fast become my conclusion that even though this is drastically unfair (mostly from the perspective of wanting to wield equal opportunities to write sneaky, entertaining posts) this has been filed under "never going to happen."

Along with the other 997 things that I thought would be a good idea.

So that's the loop closed.

Sigh.

[Edit - MA - Wow, I didn't realize a British Lady could create a full-on pout in text.]

### Michael and Language

Ok, so I'm sure it's not just me being English that has trouble understanding some of what MA is talking about half the time. Here are three phrases he uses that kinda confused the heck out of me.

"Out of pocket": Ok, so this always gets me, because in the rest of the world this means to lose money on a business transaction. MA however uses it when he's being asked for things, or hasn't done something. So I had to go look it up. Turns out that it's an old (read: OLD, old... two generations back, old) Southern expression for "out of communication".

Like who the hell is going to know that?

And besides, in the olden days weren't they always out of communication? I mean, they didn't have cell phones, or whatsapp, or fb. So why would they have a word to describe their constant state?!

"A ways out...": This is one of those like math/ maths. I kinda figured it out from context, but just makes me stop and think every time I hear it. Yep, MA, that's the glazed look I have when I'm trying to translate. Normally unrelated to the context of the conversation! ;)

"Oh snap": Yep. This one had me completely baffled. And it was during a joust on the fb page. I had to wait until he could explain what was actually going on...I couldn't figure out from the Urban dictionary definition if he was supporting *me*, or the *other* guy.

*It turned out the boys were ganging up on me.*

Sigh.

---

So during one of our many ~~arguments~~ heated discussions Ellie resigned herself to not getting anywhere with the discussion, and nodded sagely saying: "ok, Michael. Whatever helps you sleep at night."

MA thought this was hilarious. After he picked himself off the ground laughing, he made a note of it.

He has since used this phrase a total of 7 times... In a fortnight (That's two weeks for non-English-speakers!)

So after the third time, Ellie suggested that even though he found it awesome, maybe he should try a new phrase.

"Besides... it's copying!" she protested.

MA: Yeah but everybody get's something from somewhere.

Otherwise you wouldn't even be able to speak!

(Edit: you can't fault his logic!)

Ellie: Yeah, but you're using it all the time. And out of context...

*[Michael Edit – LAME!]*

---

Hey Michael, did you get that bio and stuff pulled together ok? I want to submit our SXSW application today.

MA: whaaa? Yes. Er no. Hang on.

*(Scuffling on the line as he searches for the email.)*

MA: ah yes, but... *(Pulls up email to see what he needs to do)*... It's your fault I didn't do it yet... Those two links you sent me were hilarious. I started reading through them and at 2am I'm still there going through them laughing my ass off.

Ellie: Squirrels. Rave.

MA: *You're* the one that's sending *me* squirrels in my slack channel!!!

Ellie: you didn't have to read them. And you are allowed to prioritise.

MA: whatever helps you sleep at night.

Ellie: dude - that doesn't even make sense!

---

One last one. I was talking with MA relating communication with Dr. Awesome where he was discussing his reading The Ascension Myth books. *(Michael Edit - remember to read Ellie's part in a British accent.)*

Dr. Awesome: I've been reading your books. They're like talking to you in person, only dirtier.

Ellie: I could talk dirty to you in person, but I'd be worried about your medical license.

# AUTHOR NOTES - MICHAEL ANDERLE
## JULY 23RD, 2017

First, let me say what a pleasure it is for me to type the following phrase: "Thank you for not only reading this book... But, reading it ALL the way to the end and NOW, reading my Author Notes as well."

;-)

Second, I know what you are really here for. You want to see what kind of mischief that Ell has been doing to me, lately. You are wondering what the Padawan could possibly be doing that befuddles the Yoda.

In a word? Everything (sharing later).

First, she was sick, lacking energy, falling off weight machines over in Los Angeles as she tried to get back to a normal life every time she had an erg of energy. Then, she would rail against Dr. Awesome depending on how little energy she had.

Personally, I think it had to do with how bad the caffeine withdrawals went and whether the doc realized just how out of life the prescribed regimen was sending my collaborator.

Then, Dr. Awesome became Dr. Genius. Now, you might think this was a step up for the good Doctor - but not so much. It seems with a British accent; you can REALLY make *"genius"* sound like a negative. I figured if the doc kept up with the lack of caffeine, he might get renamed Dr. Google.

As in, his doctor certificate was going to get relegated to second place behind (Ell edit: MA!) Googling for the answers. ;-)

(Michael edit to Ellie's Edit: I don't think so... I'm not the research scientist who knows all sorts of stuff, and goes out to confirm everything. That's the scientist in you.)

Don't worry if you don't understand that comment, the right person will LOL.

Finally, she had a sort of good day, and wonder-padawan started acting normal. Which is to say that she started doing more than looking out at the world as something you went and did something in, instead of watching go by as you laid on the bed or couch.

Then, shit got real.

She had two or three days of success with energy after about three weeks of nothing. Her efforts to catch up started producing results and now it was my turn to go 'oh shit, she's going to be done with the story, soon.'

*Fuck my life.*

I hadn't realized that the breather I was experiencing was just about to go down the tubes.

Perfect Padawan was about to start firing on all caffeine cylinders again (she moved herself to that mom coffee stuff which has less caffeine, and you could tell she was starting to run on premium once again and then I think she moved to something slightly stronger.)

So, my hats off to Ell Leigh Clarke as she went through a freaking horrible time in her life, and yet she has accomplished something short of miraculous that I'm going to mention here.

I'm writing this on July 23rd, 2017. Our fourth book (which is mostly Ell's efforts. We work on beats, a few major character choices and some emotional stuff) was released on July 5th, 2017.

For those who are eagle-eyed mathematicians, you will catch

that SANCTIONED (book 04) was released just 19 days before we release book 05 REBIRTH. Ell had already been writing book 05 while book 04 went through editing, so she had a small jump on the books before she went through physical hell for a while, but that is NOTHING on the fact that she fucking did it.

She released her fifth book in 19 days and I couldn't smile more for her accomplishment and I would like to be very clear.

REBIRTH is *Ell's* awesome accomplishment. She will say "ours" and to a point, it is. BUT, I want to make sure that our readers understand the Padawan deserves so much credit for the amazing results.

Right now, SANCTIONED is still a top 1,000 book in the Amazon store (#819 as I type this riding in the car from Austin to Dallas-Fort Worth) and has over 100 reviews (109).

Simply awesome!

Having said that, I can *ALREADY* hear those fans of mine saying "Well, what the hell is up with you, Michael?"

*I'm glad you asked ;-)*

I released Forever Defend on July 1st, 2017. Since then, four books have been released with collaborators including:

#2) Sanctioned (July 5th – Ell Leigh Clarke)

#3) Born Into Flames (July 7th – Justin Sloan)

#4) Shades of Dark (July 10th – Justin Sloan)

#5) The Arcadian Druid (July 19th – Candy Crum)

There are 4 more books due this month, including:

#6) Rebirth (July 24th – Ell Leigh Clarke)

#7) Storm Callers (July 26th – PT Hylton)

#8) Nomad's Force (July 28th – Craig Martelle)

AND – One more book, but in fact this is a whole NEW UNIVERSE.

#9) Quest For Magic – (July 31st – Martha Carr)

Before I explain MORE about what is going on, I want to say "I get it." I get that for many of you, it isn't about the other story lines. Many of you would rather I get the next book for Bethany

Anne out sooner. However, I chose to bring more authors into the fold (such as Ell) and frankly, I have to take time from Peter to pay Paul.

Here are my personal desires, and how they play out for the future of The Kurtherian Gambit, my own stories, and the collaborations with other authors.

**BETHANY ANNE**

She is the one that ALL of the Kurtherian Gambit revolves around (for better, or worse.) Right now, we have the following authors writing stories in the Kurtherian Gambit (In order of appearance):

1. Michael Anderle
2. Paul C. Middleton
3. Justin Sloan
4. Craig Martell
5. Natalie Grey
6. CM Raymond / LE Barbant
7. Ell Leigh Clarke
8. PT Hylton
9. Candy Crum

Here are the authors we are shepherding through to bring new series to you:

1. Amy Hopkins (AOM)
2. Brandon Barr (AOM)
3. Amy DuBoff (AOE)
4. JN Chaney (AOE)
5. Holly Dodd (Etheric Empire)
6. Hayley Lawson (Age of Madness)
7. Tommy Donbonvand (AOE)

**ORICERAN**

Now, let's add the Oriceran Universe (more on this later):

1. Martha Carr
2. SM Boyce
3. Abby-Lynn Knorr
4. Flint Maxwell
5. Sarah Noffke

## AUDIO
We are producing audio for EVERY Kurtherian Gambit / Oriceran series we have in production. So, that is a large overhead of effort.
### AUDIO for Other Authors
We have four authors running through LMBPN Publishing which we only do Audio for.
### COVERS
I'm involved in every cover setup (I allow the collaborators to project manage, but I'm part of the discussions. This includes models, costumes, concepts etc.
### BILLS
I have to make sure everyone gets paid.
### NEW AUTHORS
We (Craig, CM Raymond & LE Barbant, Martha Carr and myself) are working to bring the authors on board (new, support, etc.)
### SOCIAL
I try to stay up to date on our Facebook efforts and whoever reaches out to me.
### TRANSLATIONS
We are working to bring about German Translations if possible (test going well so far).
### EMAIL
I do all of the emails announcing new books.
Plus, all of the support for some other authors that I do ad

hoc. Now, I don't do all of this myself as Stephen Campbell is a big part of doing a LOT with this and I haven't even started to say thank you to the JIT readers, other service providers we use for website / layout / art / editing etc. we work with, communicate with and everything else that goes on to make producing these stories and getting them out to your wonderful reading hands every month..

So, I'm not personally surprised that my book dates are slipping a little. It is going to happen, unfortunately.

I just promise that I WILL complete Bethany Anne's story (21 books), Michael's story (4 books) either by the end of this year (2017) or early 2018 barring something unforeseen.

Then, I will plot out Bethany Anne's next series.

Personally, I derive a huge amount of pleasure from the success of others, and specifically my collaborators. When I see the excitement and joy they receive having busted a new record for themselves by writing with me, I'm personally damned happy.

Now, I have to admit that perhaps a little, just a little, I might be particularly pleased with Ell's success because.

She:

1. Had not read a fiction book since she was 12.
2. Was focused in a completely different area (Internet Marketing, personal success, some recent work on Story with screen writers) when she and I first spoke.
3. The Ascension Myth Series has brought NEW readers into The Kurtherian Gambit Universe. They read TAM and from there, go on to discover the other stories, including Bethany Anne.
4. Her series is a huge success, and STAYS a success. Her Facebook group is rocking it with readers speaking with her all of the time.
5. She trusted me blindly (perhaps not the most prudent decision on the face of it), but it paid off when we went

with a character that 'didn't have it all' and frankly, some worried her brokenness would turn off readers.

6. She is a scientist type person to whom I can throw sciency stuff and not only does she answer the questions, I actually understand what she is saying. That is a talent, that's all I'm saying.

Now, let's chat about a few "WTF?" moments with our favorite British author.

**That's Not Me!**

You might remember in the Sanctioned Author Notes how Ell conned me into allowing her to edit my author notes, and add some of her comments. In one of those comment adds, she made it sound as if I was going to give the wrong impression to the readers related to how often she curses.

Yet, she typed out a 'fucking' *RIGHT* in the line about not cursing!

I keep laughing about that to this day so here is…

**Ellie's Reputation, Part II**

Ellie: Fuck, fuck, fucking fuck…

Mike: And you wrote in my author notes that you don't cuss all the time.

Ellie: I hope you don't give me a bad rep in these next author notes.

Mike: <No Pause> You mean telling the *truth*???

**Gnom Nom's (The Alien Race)**

So, we were working on creating aliens a few weeks ago, needing names for some bad-ass guys. One of these names is "Gnom nom's"

Well, Ellie has a way of talking when she likes (whatever) food she is eating or talking about. She does this…

Ellie: Oh, but the food is so good! Nom nom nom…

Mike: You know that has become a fucking alien race now, right?

**Passive Aggressive**

So, Ellie and I are talking and I make some comment that leads Ellie to say "I'm passive aggressive." (Ellie edit: *being*. I said *being*. I'm not inherently any kind of aggressive!) (Michael edit to Ellie edit. *This is so wrong!)*

I happened to believe that was an incorrect description of herself and said this:

Mike: You are not passive aggressive...

Mike: You are aggressive aggressive.

Mike: For you to be passive, is like a sniper who is passive, until he shoots you.

Needless to say, she thought this was hilarious (and accurate by my estimation.)

**Ways to get Michael to Write Nothing.**

A week ago, I flew out of town to Phoenix to provide a handoff on a project that was my 'last' non-publishing / writing job. That evening, after a long day and flights etc. I'm in my hotel room and for whatever reason, Ellie is thinking it is a good idea to send me two links to funny stuff. Now, Ellie has already given me shit for having the attention span of a squirrel at a rave... And yet, she sends me two links for 'fun':

http://www.boredpanda.com/best-parenting-tweets-2017/

http://www.boredpanda.com/american-british-cultural-differences-confusion/

Not the worst, but the problem is boredpanda.com is one of those websites which has so much click bait, it is crack for your mind.

So, I'm stuck in a damned hotel room with highly questionable internet speed and I see an awesome picture of a World War II base / island that was talking about secret stuff. Now, I'm already a sucker for anything that is related to conspiracy theories and I'm off to go see about these 30 bases.

Those 30 bases are 1 PAGE EACH. Over a slow-assed internet connection downloading HUGE pages of ads...

Each picture has maybe two sentences describing what it is (nothing in depth) and it is taking me longer than a minute to get through each page.

No more taking me to task when you send me the invite to the rave, Clarke!

Giles Kurns: Rogue Instigator (2)

**The Second Dark Ages**
**\*with Michael Anderle\***
Darkest Before The Dawn (3)
Dawn Arrives (4)
**Deuces Wild**
**\*with Michael Anderle\***
Beyond The Frontiers (1)
Rampage (2)
Labyrinth (3)
Birthright (4)

BOOKS BY MICHAEL ANDERLE

For a complete list of books by Michael Anderle, please visit:

**www.lmbpn.com/ma-books/**

All LMBPN Audiobooks are Available at Audible.com and iTunes. For a complete list of audiobooks visit:

**www.lmbpn.com/audible**

# CONNECT WITH THE AUTHORS

Receive updates from Oz by registering your holo/ email
address here:
ellleighclarke.com

Facebook:
http://www.facebook.com/ellleighclarke/

Michael Anderle Social

Website:
http://kurtherianbooks.com/

Email List:
http://kurtherianbooks.com/email-list/

Facebook Here:
https://www.facebook.com/TheKurtherianGambitBooks/